ADVENTURES OF DOROTHY PICTURES

BY DOROTHY LLOYD GRIFFITHS

ABOUT THE AUTHOR

Dorothy was born in Liverpool, England and has spent the last 30 years perfecting her unique style for etchings, limited edition prints, oils and watercolours. She has had many successful exhibitions which have attracted a considerable number of private collectors literally from all over the world.

Her work ranges from botanical studies, for which she has won three medals from the Royal Horticultural Society for watercolours depicting the months of the year, through to seascapes, animal portraits, rural scenes, free flower watercolours, inks, pastels and oils. She has also produced greeting cards, illustrated books and undertaken a considerable amount of design work.

A further significant diversification occurred when Dorothy began etching, which she found to be an exciting new medium for her artistic talents. Membership of the Oxford Printmakers Co-operative, allied to Ruskin College had a beneficial influence on her early etching and laid the foundation for her increasing development and use of this art form.

Her studio and workshop is situated in Beaconsfield, Buckinghamshire, England. A beautiful idyllic countryside setting provides the inspiration for both her flower and rural scenes. She now has hundreds of etchings and litho prints on many diverse subjects, all in limited edition form. These can be purchased from her website.

www.dorothysfineart.com

First Published in Great Britain in 2009

Woodlands Studio
Butlers Court Road
Beaconsfield HP9 1SQ

www.dorothysfineart.com

ISBN-10: 978 184426 667 8

British Library Cataloguing in Publication Data.
A catalogue record for this book is available from the British Library.

Printed and bound in Great Britain by Upfront Publishing.

This is for my family

ACKNOWLEDGEMENTS

This book has come about because two of my children David and Mandy sent me on a creative writing course. Once I started I could not stop. I would like to thank my husband Bob, my children, David, Mandy, Alex and Drew who are always steadfast in their unstinting encouragement, love & help and my daughters-in-law Caroline, Lesley and Lynn for all their kind support.

I would like to thank Avril Sutton and Debbie Haines for being so supportive with their help in editing everything I have written and drawn. Also really appreciate all the inspiration from Jan Moran Neil.

Lastly I would like to thank all my friends in Covent Garden for their encouragement and enthusiasm and for all the laughs we have.

I have worked in this iconic market for many years, more than I can remember which attracts many diverse people from every corner of the world and gives the wonderful background colour which makes it so special.

Every day there is a story to tell or an unusual sight to see and it is this very lively atmosphere which I have tried to capture in this little book.

The stories are all true but I have changed the names around to save the feelings of those concerned.

Chapter One

THE MARKET

Always hold onto your dreams, perhaps they
might come true!

I have been working in this iconic Market for many years, too many to remember and feel a little as though it has become my second home.

It suffices to say, for the moment, through chance my art was accepted and I started to sell my paintings here, regularly right in the centre of London. What joy!

My life did change, I think, forever and for the better when I joined this group of completely eccentric individuals selling their amazing and sometimes ingenious creations in the heart of London in what is called the Market.

It is a long time since the pungent smell of apples and the perfume of flowers permeated the air. It had been, of course, London's fruit and veg market. Really I should say since the 16th Century but all that has long since gone. It is still easy to imagine the echoing steps of Samuel Pepys and Charles Dickens, in a way lingering on, as they pushed their way through the throngs of people, going about their business, like so many others have done throughout the centuries.

They were keen observers of life and chroniclers of their times, always needing to be amongst the ordinary people from whom they drew their inspiration. This is still the essence of the Market. I often wonder how they would react to the people who hurry by today. I think they could identify with some; others might stretch their imagination, to put it mildly.

Even George Bernard Shaw's "Pygmalion", captured the atmosphere of the Market and I would say there probably have been flower sellers like Eliza Doolittle selling her violets around the market since its inception. The tradition is still being carried on but for how much longer, who knows? All life is here as it is a microcosm of every-day life.

Buskers have frequented the area since it was a convent garden, where people sold their produce and performers made their living entertaining the crowds who congregated there.

It was into this atmosphere that through chance my art was accepted and I started selling my paintings here right in the centre of this vibrant city.

This was the start of my new journey. I had been an exhibitor at a Fine Arts Trade Fair when one of my neighbours at the exhibition, a horse painter, not a horse whisperer, although I feel he could have been, told me about the Market and said they were looking for new people and that was when I first had the idea to go and see if I would fit in.

I was duly accepted and at the beginning, I found it strange as so many seemed to have a name related to their product and they are referred to as, say, Anne Bears, who makes teddy bears. There is also Robert Clocks, Tamara Wax, Ruth Leather, Jane Ties, Harriet Scarves, Michael Cufflinks and so on. (Even Feisty Caroline really does live up to her name!) In fact the products become their names, I can honestly say I still do not know many of their surnames to this day, and I have known them a long time and consider them my dearest friends but it has really never mattered. By the way I am called Dorothy Pictures.

My favourite day has always been Sunday. On one cold January day, I was suddenly confronted by a new neighbour called Karrie Cards who made, and still makes the most extravagant cards on God's earth. We couldn't have been more different as she always thinks of herself as quite wild whereas I have always wanted to be rather smooth. Contrasts we might be but between us we gradually held the pulse of the market. Every day spent there becomes rather like a soap opera, all the romantic attachments and gossip are joyfully chewed over, laughed at, dissected and embellished but never maliciously - that would never do!

As we were setting up this morning a very tall man with a monk's haircut, come to think of it he was wearing what looked like a sack cloth monk's habit, floated through like the West Wind. He had on down to his feet the most enormous dark brown hairy cape, with a huge hood, rather reminiscent of a large brown bat. Was he a monk? Who knows but he certainly gave us a start.

Chapter Two

KARRIE CARDS

Karrie Cards is one of those people you have to say is a star. Some people look at life differently from others and that is just the way she is. Everyone who comes to gaze at her outrageously original cards gets her one thousand megawatt smile and a brief entertaining view of her life. Not that life has been roses all the way, you might say, more guns than roses but come what may, she shines through. So many people enjoy telling her their life-stories and very intriguing they are too.

Now she is a widow with two grown up daughters but she has always had this terrific work ethic, which sometimes makes her work all night to get her cards ready for sale the next day. She says once she starts work, she completely loses all sense of time and then realizes it's six in the morning and she has soon to get ready for the Market. We do try to encourage her to lead a more normal life but she has always been a bit like this. Years ago when she had an allotment, she would go out and start digging in the middle of the night. Goodness knows what the neighbours thought!

The Market is like a strange, complex group of highly compassionate and motivated individuals, all bound together by the fact they are confined and dependent on one another rather like a family. Even those who misbehave, just like the prodigal son, eventually are accepted back, reluctantly perhaps, but we always get over it, though we do all tend to have rather long memories.

We like to start the day with lots of discussion as to what has been happening when we haven't been there, after which Karrie and I usually show each other our latest creations. For me it is probably a new etching and for Karrie it will be a new design for a card. The lovely part is that we can put them out for everyone to see and usually we have lots of encouraging comments and sales but even if this doesn't happen, we still have great discussions about our ideas for new products.

We do have some wonderful customers but Karrie's are quite different to mine. She has one we call the "Gay Gravedigger", who often visits bringing chocolates and other little goodies. Some people do feel sorry for us, I don't know why, because we are very happy with our way of life. He was quite astounded when we let it slip that we had guessed about his persuasion, not that it mattered anyway. It is always hard to explain to people those tell-tale little mannerisms and we quickly changed the subject. We then continued chatting to our customers.

I sold one of my large poppy pictures. Sometimes think I should be called Mrs.Poppy as I sell so many of them.

Chapter Three

MISSING BOXES

Now there was the mysterious case of the missing boxes. First thing in the morning as we arrived for work, we were greeted with the news that Claire Crystals had lost all the boxes she keeps for her crystal jewellery. This was an unusual occurrence and very annoying for her and we immediately thought how strange it all was. How could she lose boxes? Perhaps the cleaners had thrown them away. We duly questioned them on behalf of Claire but they hadn't even been seen, let alone thrown away by them and very indignant they were and so the plot thickened. We eventually had to turn our attention to the more important task of actually getting ourselves ready for our customers and we forgot all about the problem. That is until Angus Bought-in (he doesn't make anything but buys in goods to sell) arrived and we noticed he had some identical boxes on his stand.

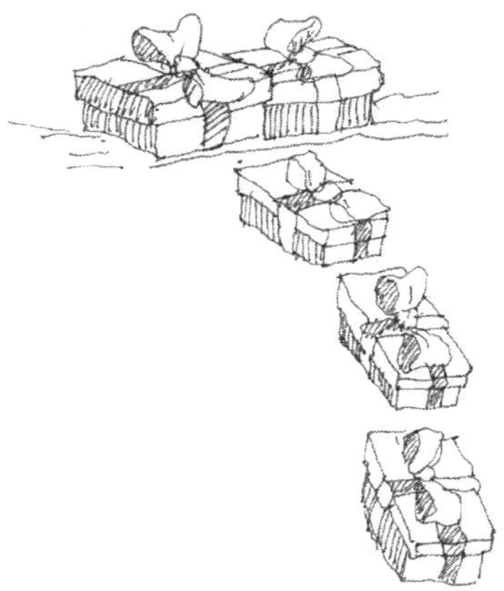

When Angus first came to the market he was what you would call a "minder". That is, he looked after the stall for the owner when he was away making his products, but now he has his own stall. He was a budding actor and always regaled us with the parts he was playing in the latest television soaps. We would spend hours looking for him on TV, only to see him for instance digging a grave in Emmerdale Farm. If you had blinked you would have missed him. It didn't matter to us, we had seen him on the television and we would all talk about it the next day. He originally came from Glasgow, and had had a hard life, so he said and came to London to help his career and I think to seek his fortune. Gradually his true character seemed to emerge and we began finding him not so amusing after all.

After he had denied everything about the boxes, we mulled over the situation but couldn't let it go. That is our problem. We cannot let anything go. We have to find out the truth even if in the end it does no good at all. But from casual questioning of Angus, he by now being off his guard, we found out the name of the company he said he had ordered the boxes from, so now we had our first clue. We had to ring them up with, I may say, a very convoluted story to find out once and for all if he had ordered the boxes in question. Of course he had not, so now we knew the truth. He of course denied everything, but the fact was he really knew that we knew he had taken them and that the whole market knew, and that was his punishment. We then got back to the very necessary job of earning our living and entertaining our public. Can I help you?

A very large muscular, completely silver Roman centurion has just walked past, covered from head to toe in silver paint. I would not otherwise recognize him as I have never seen him without the paint. He stands like a statue for most of the day amusing the passers-by, which must be quite hard when the cold wind is blowing.

Chapter Four

JANICE FAIRIES

Alongside Karrie on a Sunday is Janice Fairies, who makes the most exquisite fairies you could ever wish to see. I did ask her one day how it was that she had such unusual customers, for instance transcendental mediums, crystal healers and others who can spend ages talking about their various professions and Janice said it was because of the way she spells "fayres"!

One time she had a lady customer talking to her for what seemed like hours. In fact it turned out she was quite a famous crystal healer. Then much to our consternation, she started to twirl a crystal suspended on a thread above Janice's head. She evidently had found some special sort of electrical fields surrounding Janice. I never quite found out what they were supposed to be but it all caused quite a lot of interest, that is in between trying to serve our customers, who in fact were just as fascinated in the spectacle. Of course, Karrie had to have a go, but she sent the crystal twirling so very erratically that she was told she ought to take it easy. So that ended the session, as we thought the crystal healer didn't know what she was talking about.

Now Janice does make the most wonderful fairies, actually they are called divas, and they dangle down on glittering threads. Apparently, if you look at them long enough they give you a special feeling and then you know which one to choose. I made the mistake of choosing the same one twice and that was because evidently I had not looked at them long enough to get that special feeling.

We were in a bit of a lull and looking around when Karrie and I heard Janice talking to three customers, who had already bought some of her fairies. They looked quite normal to me, nothing special. We heard one of them saying that the fairy had made her "do naughty things". Ooh, our eyes opened wide in anticipation, our ears out on poles, hoping to find out what the naughty things were but we only caught Janice saying, "Oh they will do", in a very knowing tone. We never had the nerve to ask what the naughty things were because we had been eavesdropping but we still do wonder. Luckily or not I have not had any trouble with my fairies but who knows!

A pair of patent leather boots has just passed by with five inch wedges, twelve brass buckles to each boot. On her head the girl is wearing a red hat with two red horns so perhaps she is a little red devil, who knows?

Chapter Five

LORNA TIES

We have a mutual, very good friend called Lorna, Lorna Ties if you want me to be precise and she is in the middle of the Market on Sundays. Really she is more Karrie Cards' friend than mine. In fact they call each other sisters. They first met on the evening of the World Cup final in 1986. They of course didn't know each other at this time. Karrie was driving along, not a care in the world. Well she was eight months pregnant at the time with Tilly, who is now her daughter so perhaps not that care-free, when young football fans crashed into her car speeding on their way to the cup final football match. Fortunately, she was not badly hurt but it was Lorna who had witnessed the whole incident. In due time they were asked to go to court and that is where they met up again and finding themselves living only four roads away from one another have been the closest of friends ever since.

Realizing that they lived near to each other was an added bonus and as Lorna was already working in the Market, it followed on that eventually Karrie would join her there. Lorna likes to go to India in the winter months and has a love affair with the country. I think it's all those elephants and tigers that does it. Mind you, who would not want to go somewhere warm in January? She has a wonderful knack of spotting people who are "different".

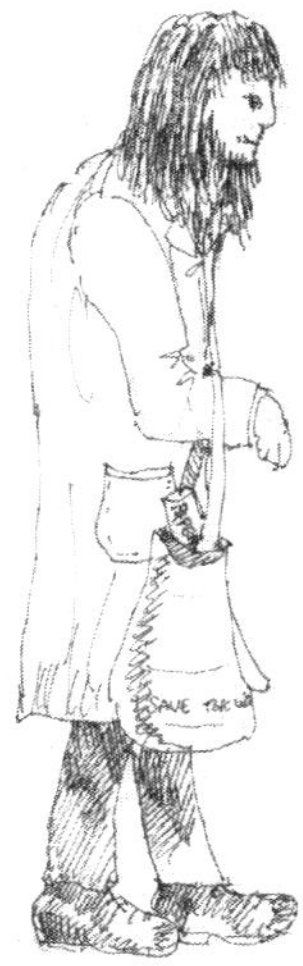

I have just caught sight of a smelly man talking to himself. He is a regular. We all smile at him and hope he doesn't come any closer.

Chapter Six

STORAGE

First thing in the morning all our products are delivered to us in trunks by Brendan, of course known as Brendan Trunks, which have been stored for us away from the Market. They are then placed in front of our stands ready for us to unpack. It is a chore to have to do this but I just treat it as a work-out instead of having to go to the gym. It certainly does keep you fit. There aren't too many fat people on the Market.

Our customers are always fascinated as to where we keep all our products and how the Market works. They are quite amazed at the effort involved in presenting our work to the public.

Then when we have finished for the day, we move the trunks from under our stands where they have been kept all day. We repack them very carefully, as they get thrown around quite a bit when being loaded on and off lorries on their way to storage. On the different days that we sell in the Market, we have a different stand. It is ridiculous to have to move around so much but that is how it works.

The storage system is operated by Brendan, as I have mentioned, who is a young Irishman and his helpers and he loves telling us stories from the Old Country, which keeps us going and makes us laugh. As he speaks to everyone in the Market he is always a great fund of gossip which I must admit we thrive on and delights us.

I hope this may give you an idea as to how the market operates. Now as you can imagine there is quite a lot of trying to juggle places to get "hot spots", which might give an advantage. I personally feel that if you display a good product, you will be seen where-ever you are, but all the same I would not like to give up my Sunday corner!

Little Iris came through wearing her dear tea cosy hat, always a smile on her face and as she does every day, she can't stop herself from looking in the bins.

Chapter Seven

WEDNESDAYS AND SALSA

I am in the Market not only on a Sunday but also Wednesdays and Saturdays. Each day that you are there you often find that there are different people next to you, who in turn become your friends. You can't avoid this, as it is essential to be able to help each other out as the day goes on and they may sell for you if you have to go and stretch your legs or to get some lunch.

On Wednesdays I have working next to me Jane Ties, Harriet Scarves and Vyada who makes jewellery from pearls. We form a square in the centre of the market along with Jael selling her crystal jewellery just around the corner. Jeweller Parish who is further along the row, with Harry the Jeweller looking on. Next to Jane is Maria the Goth who makes very stylish silver and enamel jewellery. Actually, she used to be a Goth but as she is now married with two children, this has taken the cutting edge off the Goth look but there is still a little residue. Hilary, who is at the far end, is a little bit testy at times, but full of good will.

JANE TIES

Jane and Lorna Ties were at one time partners making original hand painted ties but they decided it would be more beneficial to both of them to work separately in the Market. Their work and concept is quite different so it is an added bonus to have them both – where can you get hand painted ties with the artist on hand to advise?

We have noticed that Jane always seems to have a coterie of men who are always coming to see her, some quite famous. We all say it's to do with the ties and nothing whatsoever to do with the fact that Jane is rather beautiful. We often see her ties on television which always creates a good will feeling.

HARRIET SCARVES

Harriet and Jane are often to be seen chatting together and especially laughing, I think there is more laughter than anything else in the Market. I feel that is the over-riding feeling of our life, a sense of fun and laughter, even if your sales are bad and you have a difficult customer. They have been friends for so long, I'm sure they have forgotten how long. Harriet dyes silk velvet and makes it up into beautifully crafted scarves which take on an incredibly vibrant hue quite unlike any other velvet or silk.

Suddenly our peace was shattered by an oldish man bellowing from the window of the security offices – "Help me, save me", he shouted. We being a caring lot, felt perhaps he should be saved. Eventually he did come down and was all in one piece, so we felt he had been a little bit over-excited. Another little bit of excitement.

One dark, dank, cold Wednesday in January, a particularly miserable time of year, one of those days when you think you would like to be somewhere else, for instance the Caribbean. Then you start to imagine the warmth seeping into your body instead of being out in the cold. It set me thinking about Salsa, a Latin American dance which conjured up a lovely warm climate. So I passed the word round that I would like to go to lessons. Much to my surprise I found that there were quite a few of my fellow stallholders who could already dance the Salsa and indicated they would love to start going again. It seemed that there were a number of new minders on the Market hailing from Colombia, Brazil and Spain, in fact a very lively bunch. As I had started the ball rolling, so to speak, I next looked on the internet and found a Salsa Club, just five minutes away and it said that if you arrived before nine o'clock, you could get in free, which was an extra bonus. The club was open on Wednesday evenings which suited us all perfectly.

We finished putting away our work, which is quite a tough job as all items have to be carefully packed into trunks like a jigsaw puzzle and if not done properly you will end up with rather a lot of broken goods, which can be very annoying. Then we changed into what we thought might be suitable for Salsa dancing, nothing too fancy as everyone dresses down these days and really not knowing what to expect. As we arrived we heard an announcement that lessons were about to start, so with that we leapt onto the dance floor and lined up in rows ready to begin.

We had a wonderful india-rubber limbed teacher called Kwarmi, who came from Ghana and he impressed us greatly with his Salsa. We all had to practise the steps and as the club was downstairs and dimly lit, it was very cosy and just what we wanted after being in the cold all day. At first we were very stiff limbed, you don't realize just how rigid you are when you have been out in the cold. We were told Salsa was all to do with hip movements – oh no, I thought and I did feel a little nervous as I have two false hips but I decided I would be careful.

The music was pulsating and the atmosphere so friendly and warm. My friend Jael knew how to do the Salsa and all she needed was to sway because she already had the rhythm. However, it was not quite like that for some of us. If you stood on someone's toes, even if they visibly winced, they didn't take offence. I have to say I had some pretty large shoes treading on my poor feet, but I kept on smiling throughout, never flinching although sometimes I did have to grit my teeth a bit.

After we had mastered the rudiments of Salsa, our teacher did try and show us the Meringue, which I thought was rather overdoing things for beginners. We then had to take partners to practise with. Now I am not a teenager anymore and no-one knows my age in the Market as I purposely don't tell them. It would spoil the fun to go out with a granny now wouldn't it? I was a little apprehensive about taking partners as I thought probably no-one would want to ask me to dance but much to my amazement, no-one minded dancing with me. At first it was a little unnerving having to practise with handsome, to my eyes, young men but I'm glad to say I soon got used to it and enjoyed it rather a lot. I think they feel safe with an older woman and I do enjoy dancing.

We had to form a circle and dance with different partners with ladies moving on clock-wise, which is quite entertaining in itself. A bit like musical chairs! It is a long time since I have had to make light conversation with young men. The first thing they always ask you is your name. Now as I am called Dorothy, which I didn't think was a suitable name for a Salsa dancer, I abbreviated it to Dee. My young friend Jael also felt her name was unsuitable, so she changed it to Maxine. The next question asked was, "What do you do for a living?" Well that was quite easy as we have our own little companies, so of course we said we were business-women. Now the Salsa, unlike Garage and Rock, calls for you to be held rather close to your partner and you have to be very careful your steps don't get out of sync with the man as you just end up standing on your partner's toes and no matter what wonderful hip movement you have, it can be quite uncomfortable for all concerned. The first time this happens, it is quite acceptable but after a few tramplings it can become quite irritating and at the first opportunity the dance will end, sometimes I think rather abruptly. Our teachers were very sympathetic about this aspect of the dance and said we just had to keep on trying as it was the best way to learn.

Some Salsa dancers take it all very seriously and have amazingly intricate routines, requiring lots of agility not to mention stamina to perform. After such a session, one feels that one has to sit down for half an hour to recover.

Then again, you can get the no-hopers who have no rhythm whatsoever. Even as a beginner you can sense that they haven't a clue what they are supposed to be doing. Strangely they always think they know best and say they have been dancing this way for a long time. It is best not to argue but at the first available opportunity say you feel faint and that usually does the trick.

Then there are the ones who hold you in a grip of iron so that it is almost impossible to breathe and you spend the whole of the dance trying to get out of this vice-like grip. At first we were very grateful for anyone wanting to dance with us newcomers. Then you find yourself getting a bit fussy and carefully avoiding ones with the iron-like hold. The main thing about Salsa is that Latin American men really love this exotic dance. It is in their very bones, they have been dancing to the Salsa rhythm since they were young so they do have a head start and because of this they are very flexible and have a natural rhythm. I do have to admit that we don't quite have that rhythm.

So each Wednesday has become Salsa night for us with each week someone new wanting to join us - we're quite a merry little band. Tamara Wax, who is from Romania and works for a wax company, also helps me one day a week. She tried to ask if she could join us but as her English is not too good, it actually sounded more like "I will come with you to Salsa". As she was a newcomer, I didn't know whether she would fit it, but I agreed and she joined us the next Wednesday. She turned out to be a terrific dancer and added greatly to our little team. In the beginning she tended to wear great big woolly sweaters and boots suitable for climbing mountains but the Salsa got to her in the end and she has turned up in some really quite daring outfits. She was able to do three twirls in one which the rest of us could never master. Salsa dancing was definitely for winter months - when it became hotter even though there was good air conditioning, it wasn't quite our style to get somewhat sweaty or as ladies do, just glow. However, it did pass many a cold winter's evening and for that matter still does.

The opera singers are serenading us again so we all join in, in our own little way. What a lovely start to the day.

Chapter Eight

VALENTINE'S DAY

When February comes, the weather is usually cold and gloomy. In fact I think it is probably the worst month of all. The dim light requires the lighting to be fully on all day so it is very cheering to start thinking about Valentine's Day. It is always a boost to trade and gives us all a chance to set about designing new things, which is the whole motivation to being on the Market and earning a living. No matter how creative you are it is helpful to have a deadline. The emphasis is on hearts and roses, red of course. Everyone begins to think of new ways of presenting red roses and red hearts. Anne Bears makes her teddies with hearts on, all the jewellers suddenly produce hearts dangling down on silver chains, all very prominently displayed. In fact, there is every conceivable type of heart or rose.

Karrie always makes a very special effort with her cards, including all kinds of amusing sayings, well they amuse us! I produce etchings of roses both big and small, which always seem to go down well with the discerning buyer – after all a picture is a joy forever, at least I hope so. Jane and Lorna have some special designs with their ties. There are also bags, cufflinks, glassware and pottery to name but a few, with hearts on, each year everything seems to get better and better.

We begin to notice men with worried, haunted, distracted faces not knowing what on earth to buy for their Valentine, frantically looking. We are always very helpful to them, trying to judge the kind of thing they might be looking for. Karrie can offer to put a special message on the card, perhaps something cryptic, in an effort to be subtle.

If you don't know the person very well, it's not always appropriate to say, "You tickle my fancy", with a card having lots of feathers on! It is always the men who need a bit of help, as they never know what to say. Women know exactly what they want when it is a matter of love. Now when it comes to choosing handbags, that's a different story.

One day I had a Valentine's card left on my stall which of course caused quite a bit of excitement but in the end we decided it had been left by mistake! Unfortunately, I don't think I have a secret admirer, bit of a downer really as you always rather like the thought that someone is lusting after you other than your husband!

This year the Market's new management had erected a great number of birch tree branches, arranged to make a large heart around fifteen metres high. The branches were actually left over from Christmas displays, so we thought this was very ecologically minded of them. They then sprayed them crimson and had red laser lights shining on them making them glow beautifully. Hundreds of crystal hearts, twinkled amongst the branches and from where we were positioned, it was rather reminiscent of a red forest. The thought is there and it is unusual. I have been quite amazed at the number of people having their photographs taken inside the heart. This is, in its way, rather romantic so romance certainly is not dead. The colour of the luminous red as dusk falls is quite breathtaking and beautiful.

We looked up and couldn't really miss him. A man was passing by with cerulean blue hair, eyebrows, eyelashes and beard. We all gave him a funny look. The really strange thing is that the lady he was with was perfectly normal.

Chapter Nine

LEAP YEAR

February the 29th is always an emotive day when, so tradition tells us, it is a lady's prerogative to ask a man to marry her. This always causes a certain excitement to find out who would possibly dare to ask their partner to marry them. Four years ago, Thurston, who makes silver forks into bracelets, was asked by his young girlfriend for his hand in marriage. It all came as a bit of a shock to everyone, most of all Thurston. I have to say that after the initial surprise, they had a wonderful wedding in a marquee in a field in Wales. Tracy, his bride looked like an ethereal being in a beautiful cream dress. The dress she wore had quite an amazing history to it.

Long before Thurston met Tracy, in fact twenty years before, he had been walking near his home, minding his own business, when he saw a crumpled up wedding dress in a skip. For whatever reason and we can only assume fate, with permission, he took it out and as it was somewhat dirty he washed it four or five times and then he stored it away. The dress was hand-made in cream silk satin with a bow and a train at the back. It had long sleeves ending with a point and tiny satin buttons on each sleeve and at the neck. The intriguing point of the story is that this dress fitted Tracy, his prospective wife, perfectly. She is extra slender and very few would have been able to fit into the dress so one has to admit it was perhaps destiny.

It was a million to one chance that it would fit her, that she would like it and most importantly agree to wear it.

Thurston had made a tiara for her to wear out of silver grapefruit spoons, fitted on to sugar tongs, threaded with ribbon and ivy. Their wedding was a hand-fast pagan ceremony in which the hands of the bride and bridegroom are tied with ribbon and had to take place with fire, water and air all around. The setting was perfect and included all these elements; mountains, rivers and the barbecues for fire and delightfully they are now very happily married.

This year our friend Parish, who is a Wednesday jeweller, went into his workshop which doubles up as a shop selling his jewellery. When he looked into one of his display cabinets, he found his partner Andrea had spelt the words "marry me" in rose petals. He then rearranged them to say "yes", photographed them and sent the picture via his mobile phone to hers. What would we do without our mobile phones?

So we now have another wedding to look forward to and it just might be in a teepee! We have suggested that Parish wears one of those Ghandi style jackets. We had thought white might suit him best but as this might show up any wine stains, he will probably opt for black.

It was rather a busy day on the 29th as Karrie Cards also proposed to her childhood sweetheart. She arranged a picnic in France, scattered fifty little love cards around and presented him with one she had specially designed for him. As she had been refusing to marry him for a long time, it all came as a great surprise to him and he was quite overcome with astonishment and then happiness. This year is going to be a bumper year for weddings.

Charlie Chaplin has just passed by waving his cane so we all give him a smile. He's a busker and by the sound of the laughter gives a very good show.

Chapter Ten

THE MARKET

The way the Market is set up is a little different from most markets because we have old fashioned looking wrought iron stands, which are replicas of those used by the vendors in the old fruit and veg market. They are painted, usually not very well, a bright red and have wooden shelves giving a top and bottom part in which to display our merchandise.

Everyone, of course, has their own idea as to how their stands should look to best show off their hand-made products. Most people try very hard and have delightful displays but we do get some who have no idea whatsoever and we all think they let us down. We do try gently to advise them how to improve things but this advice usually falls on stony ground, to put it mildly. They always take it personally. We are, after all, only trying to help them to make more money. We find, from their belligerent attitude that we quickly have to change the subject and think we won't go down that route anymore!

I am lucky to have a corner spot on Sundays, which is a great help. I have been in the Market a long time and have gradually progressed to a corner. Corners mean you have an extra side to place items and it is especially useful to someone like myself, to enable me to display more of my pictures.

Next to me is Karrie Cards, who always attracts a large number of people. They just stand and adore her cards as they are so very different. Janice Fairies is next to her and the little fairies glitter so much they also attract lots of attention and so many unusual people I might add. The last one on our block is another dear friend called Misch, who is from Thailand and makes wonderful jewellery from pearls and semi-precious stones. Misch has an Italian partner called Jeremy who is always the perfect gentleman. Being Italian he likes a little wine with his lunch and always comes up and says, "Would you like some bubbles?" instead of our usual way of asking, "Would you like a glass of wine?" So from that first time of saying bubbles, it's now an integral part of our language – "Let's have some bubbles", we say. We, of course, never drink when we are in the Market as it is, against regulations and naturally we are obedient!.

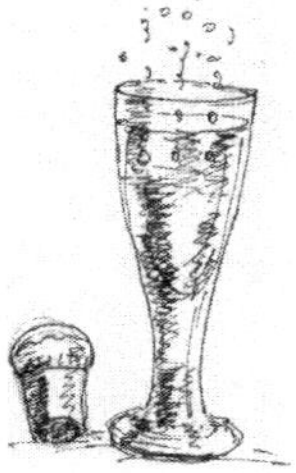

Just around the corner from my spot is Michael Cufflinks who makes "guess what?" out of silks, all beautifully displayed. He is quite like Omar Sheriff when he lets his hair grow long.

We are quite a merry little group and not because of the bubbles but we all like what we do, have great customers who make us feel good, often wanting to photograph us as perhaps we look a little strange, who knows! We all do see the humorous side of life.

Oops, Cleopatra has just floated by, the eyes, the hair, the dress a bit skin-tight but what does that matter, it's the look that counts now doesn't it?

My venture into the Market was fuelled by many things, but I think an over-riding consideration was the freedom to be able to create whatever pictures I wanted and work with. My pictures were at the time, and still are, in many galleries around the world, but I love the freedom I have of being able to make an etching that appeals to me, then hopefully to other people. I have also always loved London - having been born in Liverpool, I love cities, and was really intrigued and delighted to be able to work in the heart of the metropolis. Little did I realize how much it would change my life and introduce not only myself but also my family to such a great experience, which I feel has enriched all our lives in one way or another.

Once, I had been given the chance to study art, always having been a very creative little creature, but had been denied the opportunity to take it up. It was a long time ago and you always had to do what your father said and things were different then. When I actually did start to paint, which was much later in my life I never stopped, I don't think for a minute. It was like a cork popping out of a bottle of Champagne. This had always left me with a feeling of wanting to be with like-minded people and as soon as I arrived at the Market, I knew this was the place for me.

Had my photo taken four times today - you begin to hink you might just have two heads.

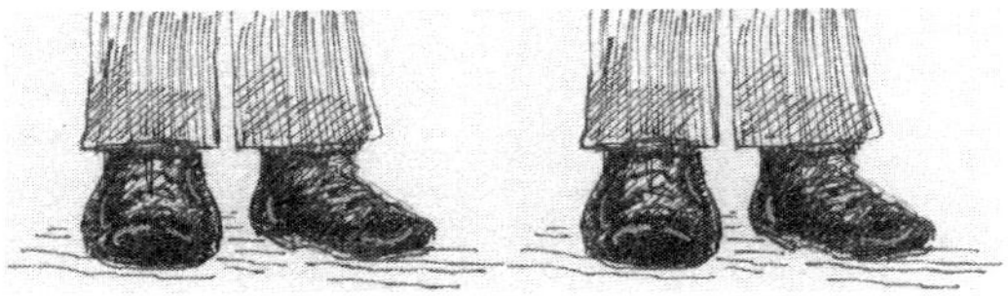

One day, it went a bit quiet in the Market and my attention was caught first of all by two pairs of exceedingly black, shiny shoes which stopped by my stall. They were shining so much you could almost see your reflection in them. Then I noticed they were attached to two oriental men wearing black suits with black ties, very tall and strong looking in that Kung Fu kind of way. Karrie and I looked at one another thinking who are they, when we saw her, a beautiful, diminutive Thai lady, who appeared to be very keen to look at our creations. Then much to our surprise, one of the men, we realized by this time they were bodyguards said, "May I introduce you to the future Queen of Thailand". It turned out she was married to the King's eldest son.

Strangely she was just as interested in us as we were with her, since we always like to find out more about the people we meet but not in an obvious way of course. She did purchase some of our goods, though actually her bodyguards paid for them and carried everything. We did feel that she would not see anything quite like our whimsical creations in Thailand. When she left us we shook her hand and we mulled over the fact that perhaps our humble creations might eventually find their way into the royal palace.

Chapter Eleven

ST. PATRICK'S DAY

This year the month of March has been extremely windy to say the least, meaning we had to metaphorically batten down the hatches as though we were at sea, otherwise our carefully made goods might have ended up on top of the church spire. Everyone then started to say it was all due to global warming but I do have to remind them that it has always been thus, March comes in like a lion and goes out like a lamb.

St. David's Day came and went. It never seems to be a big event in the Market or anything special. Perhaps in Wales it is justly celebrated. However, St. Patrick's Day, is altogether different becoming a truly lively occasion.

Then there are the hats; huge green shamrocks, green, white and orange jester hats with bells on, sparkly green top hats, I could go on forever.

Our customers' exuberance is most infectious, everyone laughing and full of joie de vivre. We always find it a very happy day and it does seem to boost our takings. I think if you are in a jovial frame of mind you are much more likely to have a good day. We, of course, all do special gifts to celebrate the day. I usually have an etching of a shamrock. There are also Irish cards, cufflinks and ties all tuned into the event. We really do enjoy designing for St Patrick's Day and it makes us forget just how desperate the weather can be in March.

Easter often comes at the end of March or beginning of April. We would always wish it to be in April as it gives us time to organize ourselves. This year at the Easter weekend snowflakes softly floated through the gaps in the glass roof onto our stalls. We don't let it dispirit us, we just wipe it off and ready ourselves to greet the public. This special weekend always brings a great many people from abroad whilst the English fly off to sunnier climes and who can blame them? Because of this large influx of visitors, even with the snow falling and slightly blizzard-like conditions, we are grateful that our customers are as stoical as us.

Easter bunnies abound, not the real thing I might add, they're usually made of chocolate but there was a very large white Easter Bunny character drifting around cheering everyone up. Lots of little yellow chicks also appear, imitation, of course and it really amazes me how these traditions keep on being replicated, year after year.

A three beaded beard man came to look at my pictures. I was tempted to ask him why but I didn't.

Chapter Twelve

THE CRYSTAL PART I

Karrie Cards had fought cancer once before but here it was back again to try and blight the life of a free spirit. The first thing is, if you are a free spirit, you don't just take notice of or do what the doctors say. She, of course, went through all the conventional treatments and got absolutely nowhere. She then went to lectures about getting yourself to believe that you haven't got it, healers who have special gifts of insight by trying to locate the trouble in your psyche, dieticians and homoeopathic doctors. I think each one helped a little. During this time the cards she made seemed to get better and better.

We were as usual discussing her health between serving our customers and feeling at this stage that things were getting worse, when Kasha, my ex daughter-in-law turned up. She had once been part of the family and was aware of Karrie's problem. She asked quite casually if Karrie would like 'the crystal'. She explained it had cured a friend's father of cancer. I was not really convinced as I couldn't see exactly how it could work but when I mentioned it to Karrie she jumped at the chance saying free spirits will try anything. So the next week, Kasha brought the crystal to the Market. It was the size of a blackbird's egg, clear with red and blue spots in it, such a pretty little thing and there were five people there who saw it in its original state. The instructions were to place it next to the skin near to the cancerous growth. As Karrie's was in her stomach she put it in her bra and there it remained for a year.

The strange thing was that it changed colour completely and went a deep opaque purple, when dark blackish lines formed on it. Once apparently it turned a dark green colour, then it became a mottled purple. Now that was all very scary. It seemed to warm up and in fact it became very hot and at one stage burnt her and with great relish we all witnessed the burns.

Now when we started talking about all this, there was great discussion as to the fact that it couldn't possibly be changing colour so it had to be carefully watched and even drawn to show the markings but change it did.

I tried to get more information about the crystal from Kasha but she had gone home to St. Petersburg, as she was not very well and it was quite a while before I saw her again. When I eventually met up with her she then told me that you could not buy one in a shop but had to go to a shaman right out in the bush in Namibia, to get such a thing.

By this time the crystal had become quite famous in our own little circle and everyone seemed to know someone who was desperate for help having tried everything else. So every Sunday we would have a look at it and then about a year after the crystal's appearance, Karrie handed it back to me. I was surprised as the crystal had become so much a part of her and her life. She said she felt really well and she didn't need it any longer, particularly as it was not doing anything! Not long afterwards she had a scan and the tumour was found to have been reduced to the size of a little finger nail so she felt she could live with that.

There he goes again, a cheerful looking man dressed and made up as a clown. He wears clown's clothes and his face has white clown make-up, red nose, mouth painted red, eyes fully painted like a clown with a tear. He has a battered black hat with a flower sticking out of the side. He wears a glittering jacket over his costume and happily shuffles along, I suppose rather like a clown would, taking photos of everyone with a toy camera, just to make them laugh. At Christmas-time he gives out little gifts to everyone he meets. He comes by on a Sunday without fail and just seems to want to be a part of the life in the Market. He always makes us smile.

Chapter Thirteen

THE CRYSTAL PART II

Nadine Minder was working on the stand next to me one Wednesday selling leather ornamental masks. She had in the past held down some very good jobs but owing to ill health, she had had to take on more casual work. Originally, she designed costumes for television dramas but as her eyesight deteriorated she upholstered clients' furniture at her home. The main problem she had was a growth behind her eye and after scans the prognosis was really bad, so bad in fact that the tumour was inoperable. I had just received the crystal back from Karrie, so I asked if she would like to try it as I had not heard from Kasha and thought she wouldn't mind if I lent it out again. Now Nadine made a band to hold the crystal and positioned it on her head nearest the growth. She could only wear the band at home because she would have felt rather embarrassed with an egg like object sticking out of the side of her head, now wouldn't you? She had already lost the sight in her eye but I just thought if the growth could be reduced to take the pressure off, then that would be great. She wore the crystal for month after month, and I asked her to note down all the different changes which occurred in it, which she did.

A year passed and we were overjoyed to be told that the growth had been reduced to the size it was when it had first been discovered by the specialist. The crystal bore no resemblance as regards to its original colour as it now had two very dark bands around it, which it certainly did not have before. The improvement in her health has enabled her to start a new career illustrating a book on homeopathic remedies which a certain Dr Pharmish is writing.

Wigs, why do men wear them? We can spot them at the other end of the Market and they are usually a dark brown or jet black. It is very difficult to serve men with a wig on as their hair becomes such a fascination that it is almost impossible to talk about your work when you can't take your eyes off their wig.

Chapter Fourteen

DR PHARMISH

We had introduced Nadine to Dr Pharmish to help her through her ordeal with her eye. She has since taken courses with Dr. Pharmish and so she knows him quite well. Mind you I don't think you could ever say you know him completely as he is an enigma.

Karrie had originally heard about Dr. Pharmish from friends who thought he was a great healer and spoke very highly of him. It was said that film stars and other famous people went to see him and that added to his aura. It is always rather intriguing to think of the famous and beautiful people having been healed by your own healer or am I being rather superficial? At that time, Karrie's husband was dying. She had her demanding business to attend to and two young girls to bring up. She was in need of some help and healing, so she went to him and consequently felt it did her a lot of good. Dr. Pharmish had been trained as a western physician and went on to homeopathic medicine as he became aware that the combination of the two disciplines was his way forward and could not practise one without the other.

His premises were called the "World of Light" and he had a multitude of different herbs and potions on display in his waiting rooms. It was a great experience to see what he had whilst waiting for him to call you and you were

never disappointed. He was very interested in crystals and had the most enormous collection of rose quartz, which at one time was piled high on the patio. I did ask jokingly if he had been mining lately! Really if they did have any kind of power, I would have been lifted off the ground and blown away. No effect at all!
I think his forte was to bring out what was really troubling you, instead of you focusing on what you thought was the problem.

I had decided to go and see him as I was suffering from an arthritic hip and thought his healing powers might help. Each time I went, I would limp into his surgery and find myself almost dancing out of there! The strange thing was he always had the effect of making you cry, I don't know why but he always did. Perhaps it was some sort of release. I don't know whether or not this applied to men but it certainly did to all my girl friends that saw him.

You are asked to lie down on a narrow couch but he never actually touches you, only his hands float above you just hovering. You certainly feel the heat going through your body. I suppose it was then that you start to unwind and your problems are washed away along with the tears. It was the most therapeutic experience possible. He was always far more interested in the mind and thought that that was the key to most problems. In a way I think I have to agree with him except that he did not believe in antibiotics which I certainly do. He always felt that if we could possibly learn to control our minds, we could cure our ailments. One of his beliefs which has always stayed with me is that tumours can shrink as well as grow for whatever reason. There is no doubt that he has some sort of power, I don't think it is just charisma. He is constantly in great demand and always has a lot of followers. He told

Karrie that she was allergic to the Market. We thought this rather silly at the time, but in the end we think he was probably right.

So if anyone has deep seated problems, we say to them, "Go and see Dr Pharmish, don't just take pills". He always manages to get out of you what the real problems you are facing are, even though you may disguise them in many forms. It is hard sometimes to reveal your deepest inner-most fears. We don't have the need to see Dr. Pharmish at the moment but have fond memories of him.

A man has just passed by looking perfectly normal, except he is wearing a short denim skirt with his shirt and tie, showing off his hairy legs.

Chapter Fifteen

THE CRYSTAL PART III

I had to ask Nadine if I could have the crystal back as I wanted to pass it on, because I heard of a very sad case of a lady, a mother of a young son who was eight years old, who found out she had only two months to live. However, with the crystal she did live for another fourteen months so it did give her a bit more time to be with him and sort out her life. This is how the crystal came to be passed from one person to another. Karrie and I actually think it is slightly radio-active as one time it set off the security alarm in a museum, which caused a bit of a scare, to put it mildly. It was touch and go at the time whether the anti terrorist squad should be called out.

The crystal has gone on from there helping so many other people. The thing is the healing process takes a long time and you have to be patient but the story of all the lives it has touched is amazing, but that is another story. Having held it a long time, I feel I am the Keeper of the Crystal and I lend it to anyone who needs it when all else has failed. I know it probably has a placebo effect but what does it matter if it actually gives someone a second chance and appears to promote healing.

Kasha just recently contacted me to ask if she could have the crystal back as she had a friend with cancer who needed it. As I had had the crystal in my possession for almost five years I felt quite sad and strange having to return it to her but I had always considered it on loan and gladly gave it back to her on the understanding that I could offer it to anyone who may need it in the future.

An Elizabeth Taylor look-alike has just walked past, her eyes and hair so amazing but she had the fattest legs ever. Someone said it must be a disease but I said that I had seen a woman just like her on television's "Diet Doctors" programme and it is all due to over-eating and no exercise! That proved "food for thought" as we all then looked at our legs.

Chapter Sixteen

BART CANDLES

Bart Candles came into our lives like an explosion. We have only ever called him Bart as that just seems to suit him. He hails from Poland, is over six feet tall and very strong looking with a shaved head. When it came to summer, we found out he had tattoos all over his body and that added to his awesome persona. I have always thought of him as a "Saviour of the Market", as his sense of right and wrong meant that he had to intervene on the side of what was right, so refreshing!

We once had a thief in our midst - incidentally, we do get a lot of thieving. This particular thief posed as a workman who had come to fix some cabinets having talked his way in, went upstairs to the office and then proceeded to open the safe. He was busy stuffing the money into his hold-all when he was discovered, whereupon he threw his bag of goodies out of the window, started to creep along the window sill, with everyone watching with their mouths open in great alarm. He then shimmied down an ornate pillar. He grabbed his bag of swag and started to sprint away. You can imagine the commotion it caused and of course our security guards were nowhere to be seen. Then it was Bart to the rescue. He ran after the scoundrel, grabbed him and the bag and held onto him until the police and security arrived. He then helped the police arrest the struggling man and was quite appalled when the thief began abusing the young constable with such obscene language, some words I hadn't even heard before. This really offended Bart and he was heard to say that had he known he was so foul-mouthed he would have given him something to be foul-mouthed about. Bart had so much respect for law and order that he had great difficulty in understanding how someone could verbally abuse the police in such a way. Then we got back to the art of serving our customers and making our living but it did give us a bit of a flip.

There was another instance when some rings went missing and with great excitement we pointed out the culprits, so Bart to the rescue again. As he approached them, he thought their faces looked a bit strange, somewhat puffy and realized that they had something in their mouths so he forced them to spit out whatever it was. That bit was not very nice. It was the rings! Furthermore he gave the culprits such a strong push that I don't think we will see them again.

His good deeds were legend and we always cheered him when he sorted things out but he was so modest and always said he was only doing what he considered was right. One thing though, we encouraged him to grow his hair, as he was obviously not bald and so after a while he did just that. Never interfere with anyone's hair, that is the thing I have learnt, just keep your thoughts to yourself. He did eventually grow his hair and then a beard which he plaited. His hair grew so long he had to keep it back with an Alice band and he looked like the Old Man of the Mountains, none of which suited him and secretly we decided we all preferred Bart bald but we couldn't very well tell him could we?

Chapter Seventeen

DARLING TILLY

Just lately Karrie has been trying to take life a bit easier, so her daughter Tilly has been helping her to design the cards and also to sell them. We call her Darling Tilly because that is just what she is. She has proved herself to have a natural aptitude for making extra special cards and daily they grow more exotic, much to the delight of her customers. I feel it is the attention to detail which is quite amazing and makes them so unusual. She is married to Roie who is a musician who at one time worked with his brother in the Market. It was a way of financing themselves whilst they were launching their careers in the music world, which as we know is a very hard industry in which to succeed, rather like the art world. Both brothers are very musical as is their father, who is a well-known singer and they want to follow in his footsteps as regards a musical career. Although it has been difficult, they have now managed to forge their careers and are now getting a considerable amount of success.

CHERRY

Now Tilly has quite a remarkable looking sister-in-law called Cherry, who appeared on the Market it seemed at first without us realizing she was there. I think this is because she has a somewhat quiet personality. To make up for this, she always dresses in a most unusual way and you might say a trifle bizarre. In fact everyone who sees her gives her a second glance for which she seems to be quite oblivious.

Today I would describe her appearance as Chinoiserie, anyway a Chinese style of sorts. It is a very cold day, with a foul wind blowing through the Market, so her outfit in that respect is very adequate. She has on four layers of dresses, a short one on the top, then the others each have different lengths, terminating in jeans and big fur boots. Over these toning dresses she has on a long Chinese black satin embroidered jacket, edged with black fur and all very beautiful. On her head she wears a fur hat over hair dyed a sort of darkish purple, which matches some of the embroidery in the jacket and her dresses. Round her neck are countless necklaces with jewellery dripping from her fur hat and her ears. Little teddy bears are pinned to her frocks. Bracelets and rings of every description adorn her hands.

Recently she happened to be near us so this was the perfect opportunity to try and understand what was behind this extravagant exterior. Then she began to tell us how when she was in her twenties she suddenly became agoraphobic and so for most of this time she suffered and just about never went out. We, of course, could hardly believe it now and we were fascinated to find out how she had changed. Suddenly, for no reason, it lifted off her completely and she was able to resume a normal life and with this came this wonderful outward-going personality. She now finds it hard to believe that at one time she could hardly leave the house.

Most of her twenties were in fact lost because she could never travel anywhere and so she led this very secluded life at her parents' home. Being a parent myself I wonder what her mother and father went through. She said that one day the feeling just disappeared and she felt she could once more go out and meet people. Then followed this extravagant dressing, seemingly she was unable to stop adding little bits to her costumes or her clothes. Every time you see her she looks entirely different, with a wonderful collection of wigs, perhaps one day dressed as a Russian doll or at Christmastime very fairy-like.

We asked her if she had ever been interested in becoming an actress, as we feel that perhaps this is what is trying to get out and acting may indeed be her forte. She told us she is now a singer in a girl band and we have all decided that next time she is appearing in London we shall go and see her. What we always try and do is give lots of encouragement whenever we can.

I put on display my new peony picture (I do love peonies) and it sold. I do sell a lot of pictures but when I sell a large painting, I feel quite thrilled that I am helping to decorate someone's home.

LIFE PASSING BY

When we are not worrying about the weather or lack of sales and we don't have much to do, we tend to survey all the people passing by. We often comment on the importance of religion in people's lives.

A group of Jewish youths came along, soberly dressed in black suits, all wearing very wide fedora felt hats. Now the hats must be of some significance, I can't imagine what! Then shortly after, we noticed a Muslim family with the father striding ahead and the wife dressed in black, her head completely covered with black gauze, presumably so that no-one except her husband might look at her face. Next we had a group of very smartly dressed Sikhs complete with colourful turbans and beards tightly wound round their chins. Then came a Buddhist monk in saffron robes, actually more like faded orange, with an ethereal look on his face. There was then a priest from the local

Catholic church dressed in grey and black. We even noticed a small Indian gentleman with a gold ornament fixed to his forehead. We wondered what it was fixed on with, perhaps super-glue but we thought that it must be of religious significance. We often reflect on what a variety of people we have passing by and what would it be like if there were no religions. Life would be a lot less colourful and we certainly wouldn't have so many interesting people to look at.

This is the collar every fashion conscious fighting dog should have.

Chapter Eighteen

THEM AND US Part 1

It is easy to imagine with so many diverse characters in the Market, naturally there would be misunderstandings between the management and the artisans. The management tries to impose petty regulations and restrictions, which are never fully thought through, as though it is a school for naughty children, even though we pay a high price for being there - in all weathers! Those of us who have been there a long time have seen it all before and know which things will work and which will not, which I suppose can be irritating for them. At one time we had a management team who actually did care about the Market and the people who worked there and genuinely tried to help them. They took an interest in all the different crafts and the makers themselves and knew everyone personally which is of great benefit in any organisation. Since property prices in London have become astronomically high, the Market has just become a commodity to be bought and sold at will. Each company has their own agenda, which could be to push up the profits regardless of the quality of the merchandise, then sell it on to make bigger and bigger profits. Our one light at the end of the tunnel is the Trust which governs how the market is run and it does from time to time try and redress the balance. Because we have been here for many years, we have seen management teams come and go, trying to impose their will on us and in the end they are marched out with security guards hard on their heels. The last manager came as a temp and then she was promoted to Market Manager with quite disastrous results for the quality of the Market. To be fair, she was to a certain extent following orders and new traders are not always truthful.

Someone wearing the largest pair of black ladies trousers I have ever seen passes by. You wonder where they get them from.

MUMSY

One fairly regular customer is an Asian lady, who could only be described as imperious. She is tall and statuesque, and initially someone thought she was a man in drag. As she calls herself "Mumsy", we don't think she is a man. She comes by accompanied by her beautifully and immaculately dressed husband, who patiently waits for her without complaint. She is further accompanied by several minders, who pay for everything and carry her purchases. One of the unusual things about her is that she is laden down with gold jewellery. She has three solid gold amulets about an inch thick around each ankle. On her wrists there are even more and each finger has a large ring on it. In addition to her ear-rings and necklaces, she has a huge diamond in her nose. It is so big you keep trying not to look at it but your eyes are constantly drawn back to it and you wonder whether it is real.

Her hair, like a bushy halo, is dyed a lurid henna red and the make-up on her face gives her a gruesome appearance. With this striking look, we can spot her as soon as she and her entourage enter the Market. Karrie and I brace ourselves and wonder what she wants to buy today. When she first came we were very interested just looking at all her jewellery and so we gave in to the haggling that ensued but as time has gone on we have become a little tired of Mumsy so we ready ourselves for her and don't give in to being haggled. "Would you expect a discount at Harrods?", is our favourite question? We are never rude to her but she does try our patience as she likes to treat us as inferiors, which is always a mistake and just hardens our attitude towards her. However, she must like our products as she still comes back. How her husband puts up with her is a mystery!

The fire fighters are back with their special fund raising day of races but so very, very noisy. Had to ask them to keep the noise down as we couldn't hear ourselves speak. We just couldn't have that.

FLOWER SELLERS

Ever since I have been on the Market there have been flower-sellers and they certainly are as colourful as their flowers. They tell me they have been selling flowers here for a very long time, passing the business down from one generation to another. They are usually to be found dressed up as you might imagine "My Fair Lady's" Eliza Doolittle to have been, with big straw hats with floral trimming and little posies in a great wicker basket. They are Londoners through and through, but I think that they could have been descended from Romanies as they are quite dark skinned and somewhat gypsy-like. They say if you buy a posy you will have good luck but sometimes they can be quite aggressive and get cross if people don't wish to buy. Once you get to know them, however, they are really very sweet and keep handing you flowers to give you luck - it's just as well to be on the good side of them, I wouldn't like a curse. They are after all only flower sellers but there is always that very slight superstitious feeling that they just might have special powers.

Recently, the mother of one of them died and they held what can only be described as a lavish funeral. I was told there was a carriage with two horses pulling the cortege with a procession of people walking behind. All the women had large black hats with full veils so I suppose you could call it a grand East End funeral rather Victorian in a way.

A lovely lady has just stopped. Scottish, I must presume as she is dressed in a long tartan coat, tartan trews, tartan boots and tartan beret with a feather cockade. Delightful sight.

Chapter Nineteen

MY STORY

I was always a very creative child but growing up in Liverpool as a war baby, there naturally wasn't a great deal of interest in the arts in the aftermath of the Second World War. Certainly to have a career in anything to do with painting pictures, especially being a girl, was almost unheard of. Being an artist was called being Bohemian and that's just what I would have liked to be.

The part of Liverpool I lived in was very pleasant and quite typical of the time with virtually no crime to speak of. Perhaps that was because there were always fathers in the houses, who would, if they found anyone outside their house misbehaving, not hesitate to shout at them and if caught you knew you would be in for a hiding. Not that I did anything like that! I have absolutely no recollection of any child in a home where there wasn't a father.

Everyone seemed to have such pride in the appearance of their houses and the absolute must was to whiten your door step every day. I wonder how many people now even mop their step daily. I think the cleanliness really emanated from the fact that antibiotics had not come onto the scene and all you had was basically soap and water and of course, herbs, to ward off germs. Most people would boil anything that could be boiled and all surfaces were kept as clean as possible, including the airing of bedding and carpets. The down-side was that if you were not as particular as you should be everyone knew and would talk about you, but generally speaking everyone kept up their rituals. The strange thing was everyone addressed each other formally, for instance Mrs Rothwell or Mrs Maud and I still called them this thirty years later. Even when invited to call them by their Christian names I always felt I should address them formally, I suppose old habits die hard.

The gardens were a joy to look at and our next door neighbours had wonderfully colourful flowerbeds reflecting all the seasons. With Spring came the Daffs, as they called them, together with Tulips and Primroses, all having been carefully planted. Summer beds were always full of annuals, raised from seed and hardened off ready for planting out. French Marigolds, Salvias, Purple Asters, Pansies mixed in with perennials such as Blue Betty, Delphiniums, Pinks and Carnations were a must, even Bleeding Hearts, all the old English plants. When Autumn came, up popped the Gladiolii, Chrysanthemums and Dahlias, such a riot of colour. Dahias now seem to have gone out of fashion but they then seemed to be very popular I suppose because they gave a vibrant colour late in the season. In fact I really like painting gardens and did teach flower painting for quite a number of years.

Funnily enough at this time we had a dog, mongrel, of course, I can't recall any pure breed dogs around at that time. He had some Collie in him so we always thought of him as a Sheepdog. He had a friend, a little brown doggie, who waited outside for him each morning until we let our dog out. Off they would trot together, we never found out where they went to but there were never any complaints about him and he duly returned when he wanted to. Can you imagine that today? I should think after about half an hour he would be rounded up and put in a dog pound.

As I said, there wasn't a great deal of encouragement for an artist, wanting to be a Bohemian and to paint pictures all day, apart for them to say that she does draw well.

I always had this dream which I kept within me. Though I did come from an artistic family on my father's side. One of my uncles claimed to have painted with Augustus John who he said came with some very important people from Liverpool to paint at his house and lake up in the wilds of Snowdonia. By the way it is very beautiful there and I have since done a few paintings of it myself. Of course, we have no proof and it was probably just a fable, to put it kindly. Also the story goes that some ancestors sculpted the friezes for St. George's Hall in Liverpool, which as you may or may not know is a very important building. All this fuelled my desire to paint pictures. Unfortunately I had to wait a long time before it actually happened. It was not long after this era that everything changed and when the sixties began it was just a little too late for me.

At the age of fifteen, the time came for me to choose my career. I wanted to go to Liverpool Art School but my father, being a business man, did not agree and he thought I should take a Business Studies course and become a secretary. I was as you can imagine horrified but no matter how I pleaded, sulked, had tantrums and wheedled, I was not allowed to go. Instead I went to Secretarial College and learnt how to be a good secretary. I did go around like Lady MacBeth for a long time and I must have driven everyone quite mad.

I did try again a year later and could have gone to Art School, but my father died, so perhaps he knew something

I didn't know. That was it, I had to get a well paid job as I now had myself and a widowed mother to look after. Inside I was very bitter but I never lost sight of one day being able to make a living from being a painter.

My life went on but I always had this dream to fulfil myself as an artist. Always hold on to your dreams, they are so important and never lose sight of them as it's so easy to let them go. I married a charming man, had four lovely children and my life joyfully revolved around my family so there was very little time for anything else. It wasn't until my youngest child Drew began school that the idea came to me to try and realize my dream.

I had never been taught a great deal about perspective or any of the technical aspects of art even though I had passed my art 'O' level exam. I think it was judged on your ability to draw more than anything. I didn't want to be a Sunday painter and right from the start I wanted to be able to see if I could make my living as an artist.
It took time but I persevered; my four young children were very important to me and so I had to fit it in with family life. In addition, at that time I had to look after an exceptionally naughty dog, home and garden with my husband working in London, frequently travelling around the world on business.

Every day when I had the time, I continued to teach myself and had to be very disciplined, it's the only way. Time is so important. Some time later I happened to be sitting in the local barber's shop, not getting my hair cut, thank you very much but waiting with my sons to have their hair cut, when I noticed that there was a completely empty window to the street. I suggested to the barber, Mr Harding - he was a twin, the nice one, his brother was always the grumpy one, so you see we are what we are - that it might be to our mutual benefit if I displayed some of my pictures in his window and he could take a worthwhile percentage of anything he sold. He agreed to this.

This was the start of my real artistic journey which has not stopped from that very day. People bought my pictures and everyone seemed to want to help - each week it was really thrilling to see what had been sold and to be able to try out something new.

As my children were beginning to grow up, they were all a tremendous help in my new business. They assisted me in my humble studio in a thousand ways and without this, my dream could not have become reality. Even now they are full of ideas as to how I should progress and their help and good will is of the most utmost importance to me.

I considered my pictures would sell better framed so I put an advertisement in one of the local shops asking for someone to make frames. Along came Charlie who was a retired postman looking for something to do. In the end he became my right-hand man and almost a surrogate granddad to my children. Between us we taught ourselves how to make frames. It was very hit and miss at first, the blind leading the blind is more apt. As I mentioned before, the family had a very naughty Labrador dog called Dan who we all adored and of course, Charlie came under his spell. He loved the dog to such an extent that in later times, when he was undergoing major operations for cancer, we all felt that it was Dan that kept him going. We used to take Dan to the hospital, so that Charlie could see him through the window, just to cheer him up. He would insist on getting out of hospital as soon as he possibly could so that he could take the dog for a walk even though we tried to stop him as we thought he was too weak.

Eventually, I decided to try the London Exhibitions and was lucky enough to get acceptance to all I applied for. I drew everything of interest where I lived, almost in a frenzy. I mastered perspective, also pen and ink work which came very easily. Watercolour I found a bit more difficult but in the end managed to master it fairly well and the same went with oils.

At about this time I started painting flowers - in fact at one time I wondered if I should become a botanical artist but decided against it. I felt it was too restrictive. I was lucky enough to have exhibitions at the Royal Horticultural Society, which I felt was a great honour. The botanical work exhibited there is truly breathtaking. I continued at such a pace, I suppose I felt I had to make up for all the time lost and even now I still have that feeling. I am continually thinking about a new idea or process to follow almost as though time is running out.

I had always loved the look of etchings, you either love them or they mean absolutely nothing to you. The only place I could find to pursue this little dream was in Oxford. I then joined the Oxford Printmakers Co-operative. You had to be able to etch as it was not really a teaching establishment so I just pretended I could do it. I went every Tuesday, always being back at home for three o'clock for my children coming home from school, just delighted to be able to learn this ancient craft. I was like a sponge, taking everything in and eventually a second-hand press came up for sale. I thought I would ask the bank for a loan to buy the etching press, as I was very keen to have everything self-financing. I fondly remember going to see the bank manager all dressed up in my best designer coat, which is always a great boost to morale. In those days it was possible to have a chat with your bank manager not an alien from another planet. He listened to my story and agreed to lend me the money. My coat must have done the trick and I duly purchased the press. What a great day! I still have it and when I think of the incredible amount of work I have produced on this old press over the years, what a bargain it was!

From then on, I couldn't stop! I moved out of the garage, which had been my studio for some time and into a local industrial unit. I had been working there for about a year when Lord Burnham, our local Laird, offered me use of a redundant calving shed on his estate. This was to become a wonderful studio. It was huge, about 2,000 square feet and it had beautiful foals and calves in the fields on one side and lovely rural pastoral views of trees and cottages all around. This was and still is a great inspiration for my work.

Throughout this time my children and husband helped me; my husband with business, David with sales, Alex became an expert picture framer, Drew and Mandy, my daughter, assisted all the time at the trade fairs, particularly at Covent Garden and other selling venues. Their help and love has been unconditional and continuous. I should also mention friend Jen who has been with me non-stop for many years. My art then progressed into a thriving business and that is when I started to attend fine art trade fairs, which is when I met the horse painter and where I began this unusual journey.

Bright green fishnet legs have just passed by with large holes in them. There is no stitch in time saves nine any more.

Chapter Twenty

SUMMER OUTING

Once May is here we look forward with great relish to hopefully a warm Summer. The joy of not having to wrap up as though going to the Arctic Circle really is almost like a lily blooming or coming out of hibernation. Everyone seems to look so much slimmer and neater as we shed our thermals and great coats. Our minds then naturally start to concentrate on enjoying ourselves, not that we don't in any case but the question always arises, "What about a Summer outing?"

Now there is one thing that we all enjoy and that is a day away from our work, just to completely relax. One of the places we like to go to is the seaside, not to a large seaside town but our preference is to a rather old fashioned out of the way place like Littlehampton on the South Coast. We need someone to organize these outings as we are all highly creative individuals and find that part of life rather difficult. It has often fallen to Adrian Photos as he likes sorting us all out.

We usually have our outings on Mondays as that is our day off from the Market and we find then that we don't have to worry about everywhere being very crowded. As there are usually about thirty to forty of us we like to hire a bus so that we will all be together and it's certainly more fun that way.

This time he arranged for an open top bus to take us to Littlehampton. Amazingly it has never rained on our outings and it never occurs to us that the weather might not be good. We have more of a problem with sun burn than anything else and when the wind gets up, we all look as though we are in a wind tunnel or affected by gravity. Unbelievably we had managed to prise out quite a nice sum of money from the management for Champagne and strawberries to consume on our way to the coast.

I always ensure that we have proper Champagne glasses as I feel it doesn't taste quite the same out of plastic cups. One cannot go on a bus trip without the champers.

My friends and I like to sit at the front on top deck, so we were the first ones on board. As usual we were rather late starting off, there being several missing individuals who couldn't find the bus, so we thought it best to start on the champers. Whilst waiting for the others, we came to thinking that we could have had a really great party just sitting on the bus on the piazza by the Market drinking Champagne, eating our strawberries and chatting to all the passers-by.

I have forgotten to mention that we usually like to dress up for these occasions and the more daring the outfit the better and this time in particular we decided to wear hats. It is never stipulated that they should be outrageous but that is always how they end up. This time the hats were sensational in brilliant colours with lots of flowers decorating them. To match these, I did notice that there were rather a lot of strange and colourful costumes. There were wonderfully startling South Sea Islanders with huge grass skirts and garlands of flowers but these got a bit frayed by the end of the day as they had been used as everything but a skirt. Some people just came in their normal clothes but even that was a sight for sore eyes as quite often they were even more outrageous than the costumes. Brightly coloured hair extensions, amazing outfits, huge boots, that is their usual dress. By the time we did set off, we were rather a merry crowd and I think that our journey across London caused quite a few turned heads, especially as the laughter drowned the London traffic but we were never rowdy. We did feel it cheered everyone up.

The bus is always rather slow as we like to take the scenic route where possible, as we are not worried about time and we enjoy surveying the scenery as we go along. When we pass cows there are great “oohs”! In fact for all animals there is the same reaction, as working in London most people don’t see them very often so they are greeted with great interest. We trundle through all the lovely

English villages where everyone waves with smiles and cheers as we pass by. Dogs sometimes bark, cats run away, little children wave but it is always a happy event. What a truly beautiful country we have.

When we reached our destination, we were received with great generosity of spirit because as we descended from the bus, it was almost as though aliens had arrived from outer space. We were questioned as to where we had come from and everyone seemed delighted to talk to us. Personally I think it was mainly out of curiosity as it isn't every day you see such a brightly coloured bunch of people. Shopkeepers really liked us as we are all big spenders, well relatively speaking that is, but we did take quite a few gifts back home with us, which was rather interesting to say the least as they were similar to the goods we ourselves make!

Happily for our day off work, it was a beautiful sunny day, so Adrian's next job was to round us up and take us all down to the sea. I have always noticed on these outings everyone seems to go off in different directions and then can't find each other and we spend most of the time looking for one another. We eventually arrived at the beach on this amazingly very warm day. In fact the heat took us by surprise as the weather forecast had not predicted such high temperatures. After choosing just the right spot for us, we settled down and out came the "bubbles" again as the hot weather had made us thirsty. When the Champagne eventually ran out, plastic bottles of frozen cocktails and G & Ts appeared, by now defrosted and deliciously cold. Perfect for our day at the seaside.

We were much amused by the ingenious hat which keeps the face from getting sunburnt.

When we were all settled, Adrian announced there would be a sand castle competition and this became quite competitive, with a little skullduggery on all sides I thought. As they are such creative people the sandcastles became more and more extravagant and Champagne bottles, empty of course, were used to prop up the turrets. They even appeared as cannon to repel invading marauders. There was great excitement looking for shells or anything that could be used to enhance these exotic fabrications. They did look somewhat wild as you can imagine. Eventually time was called and the judging began which everyone automatically thought was unfair as they all thought theirs was the best, but as there were several prizes no one really minded and in the end it was all just good fun. I do marvel how there is someone who thinks of getting prizes and wrapping them up, just to make the day more enjoyable for everyone.

After all the fun and general running around, some wanted a dip in the sea to cool off. At first I was slightly aghast at the thought but many did take to the water as it was so warm whilst others happily managed to paddle their toes.

Being at the seaside we decided we had to sample the local fish and chips. In fact there seemed to be a constant smell of chips and vinegar wherever we went. We ended up in an old fashioned emporium that hadn't been altered for many years and set amongst little neatly painted boarding houses. Again everyone seemed delighted to talk to us to find out I think where we had come from. The fish and chips were delicious, particularly as I don't normally eat them anymore and just as I remember them from my youth. There was a fair ground with merry-go-rounds, dodgem cars, ice cream vendors, fruit machines and candy floss stands, all quite traditional and charming.

Eventually after everyone had had a doze, argued about what time we were leaving, had a ride on the dodgems and looked at everything it was possible to see, we were all once again rounded up by Adrian. I do feel Adrian has missed his true calling as he should be a professional organizer. With glowing red faces, we then departed on our journey back to London. It has always been our practice to sing all the way home but why is it that you can only remember the first two lines of any song? Every time we are on the bus we think we ought to supply song sheets but we never do. Well fortunately we had on board Evo, who we call Tall Evo as she is quite statuesque, resembling a model, with a wonderful singing voice. My everlasting memory is of Evo standing up on the top deck of the bus singing "House of the Rising Sun" complete with actions, whilst Karrie and I tried to pull her down before she was decapitated by the branches of the London plane trees. She was of course a little on the merry side, as we all were. We arrived back in the centre of London having thoroughly enjoyed our breath of fresh air at the sea side and this led to us wondering how to persuade Adrian to take us on another trip. Perhaps we'll have a boat trip next time.

A man with a pin sized head and a huge body came walking by. He had a pig tail – fancy having a pig-tail with a bald head.

Chapter Twenty One

WENDY MINDER

Wendy Minder entered our midst one morning startling us with her exotic appearance and that is saying something because by our standards we witness so many unusual sights that it not so very easy to distract us from our work but we did think she was something special. I would estimate her hair was about a foot high and full of very bright extensions with dreadlocks mixed in. She arrives fully colour co-ordinated, so when for instance she chooses turquoise, her eye make-up, hair and clothes are brilliantly turquoise, but when it comes to her boots, they are always black clumpy three inch wedges. When she wears magenta and pink she completely changes her style but again is a sight to behold. She is so colourful, customers keep talking to her about her appearance and ask if they can take photos, so much so

I feel it is to the detriment of her sales. She has been working for a Brazilian girl called Christina Bags, who makes very unusual bags and mini-skirts out of her own comic-strip material. Christina does not mind at all when Wendy wears the mini-skirts over her own outfits, because it all adds to the amazing effect. The material is very interesting and so is Christina and being Brazilian, she is quite fiery. If the management do what she considers are silly things, she goes straight up to the office ticking them off, none of your English reserve for her.

We took a great deal of interest in Wendy and soon found out that she was really a would-be actress. She had her own little act which centred round her dancing with a sixteen foot snake called Suzie Snake (I'm only joking it was just called Suzie) and she was often invited to perform at corporate functions in grand hotels. Suzie was her second love, her first one being her boyfriend who she was very fond of but that was until something rather strange started to happen. She began to tell us about a girl who resembled her a little and had even started to dress like her. I suppose you could call her a kind of groupie. This particular girl always seemed to arrive where ever she was and attached herself to Wendy. At first we thought this could hardly be possible as Wendy's clothing and look was so completely bizarre. We didn't say this to her face as it would have been a little unkind but every time we saw her she told us she felt as though she was being cloned. At first she was a little flattered but then noticed that the clone was taking rather a lot of interest in her boyfriend. Things were getting serious. It all came to a head one morning, when we found her crying, so we had to get the whole story from her, even if it meant being late setting up our work - affairs of the heart are sometimes more important. Her boyfriend had told her he wanted a ménage a trois with the clone. This state of affairs needed a lot of mulling over, as it was very important to give her the right advice. We really felt he was not a nice person to suggest it in the first place but there is little good in telling that to someone who is in love since they cannot bear to hear it.

After much thought, the decision was made not to agree to his request because he might end up liking the other one better than you - then where would you be? After all this, we carried on setting up a trifle late, I'm afraid. But in the end the decision was completely taken out of Wendy's hands, as the clone just moved in and Wendy was compelled to move out with her Suzie. This was very distressing and unfair to her, but she still had her second love!

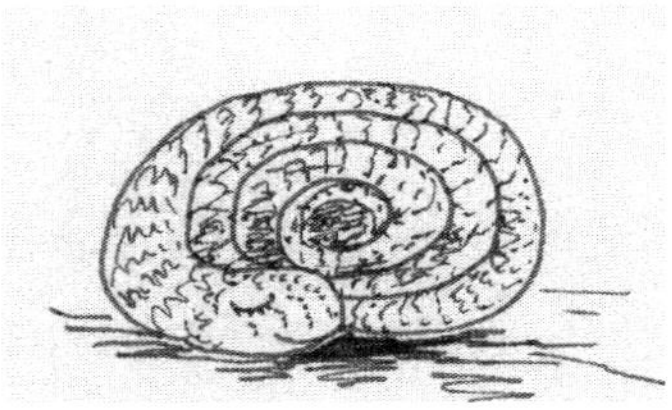

She was then offered a part in a show in Denmark. I don't think they have anything at all quite like Wendy Minder there and we believe she was very successful but whatever happened to Suzie, I don't know. We never did find out

A young opera singer, with the most hauntingly beautiful voice has been serenading us. Her notes are so pure and perfect it did bring tears to my eyes. It makes you stop whatever you are doing just to listen. She is just a slip of a girl, with a heavenly voice, making the whole performance appear to the onlooker completely effortless.

Chapter Twenty Two

HARRY THE JEWELLER

Harry the Jeweller has been in the Market since it was redeveloped, so you could say there is not such a great deal that he doesn't know about. We always put the "the" in, it's never without and almost like a title. He has seen many come and go, especially our management. If you have only heard half a story that is going round and you want to hear the rest of it, he is your man. He is invariably to be seen polishing his jewellery, so everyone feels obliged to talk to him and that's how he hears all the gossip. As a goldsmith, he has wonderful jewellery and everything is beautifully polished and displayed. The polishing is almost a continuous process from starting up to closing down, he just never seems to stop.

He is, however, such an unconventional person, you could say he's a true hippy. At one time though he lived in a squat and that is how he met his wife. To see them now married, as bastion of respectability, there is hope for everyone. In his hippy days he travelled throughout India and onto Thailand, long before it became a holiday destination and I don't think that way of life has entirely left him. I say that as the other day five of us stallholders Harry, Jane Ties, Lorna Ties, Peter Bears and myself decided to attend a meeting, which was to be held in a very grandiose place, actually it was the Masonic Temple where all the Market Big Wigs were going to be, all suited and booted, making very important speeches with lots of networking afterwards, so they said. Harry turned up in sandals showing all his toes, as he said his feet had been hot and then I thought why not, why put up with hot feet? Apart from me, I don't think anyone actually noticed. I had tried so hard to give the impression of a sleek, with-it business woman but I thought we are all so different what does it matter!

There are many jewellers in the market and there is such rivalry among them, frequently checking to see what the others have sold and furious if they have sold more, but still it is good to have competition and it is always friendly - really it is!

Teenage years are always difficult, particularly hairstyles

ORDER OF THE MOPSES

At this point, I must tell you a funny tale, well I thought it was very amusing. Our little group were rather early for the important meeting and having sampled the free pens and everything that was on offer, we decided to look round the Masonic Museum and as usual we wanted to have a look at everything on display.

Amongst all the exhibits we noticed that there were numerous statues of pug dogs. China pug dogs under ladies arms, pug dog peeping out from under their skirts, pug dogs on leads, little china statuettes, ad infinitum.

They were so fascinating that we asked the Curator what their significance was - she didn't take any notice of Harry's toes - but she guided us to an explanation of the pug dogs. We read that in Germany in the 1730s the name for a pug dog was "mops" and a Masonic order was founded called the "Mopses" when both male and female members had to give allegiance of fidelity and love. It was quite rare at this time for women to be included as equal partners in the Masonic Lodge. There was an unusual initiation ceremony which entailed being blindfolded and kissing the rump of a pug dog. "What! A pug dog's bottom?" We all gasped in horror at this and then read on that it was not a real pug dog but a wax statue with a cloth tail. What a relief that was but it didn't stop us amusing ourselves saying, " Kiss my Mopses".

What a strange initiation ceremony that would have been! I thought, trust the gang, out of all the intriguing, wonderful and unusual exhibits of silverware and memorabilia they had to alight upon the story of the Order of the Mopses. We did think the Masonic Temple was an amazing example of art deco style and the marble was absolutely exquisite, the building financed by donations to commemorate those lost in the First World War.

HATS

Hats are definitely coming back into fashion. If you think about it, in the not too distant past everyone wore a hat because a very large percentage of heat is lost through the uncovered head. Sometimes, they did not even take them off when indoors, I suppose it was because of the cold again. Then hats became generally unfashionable.

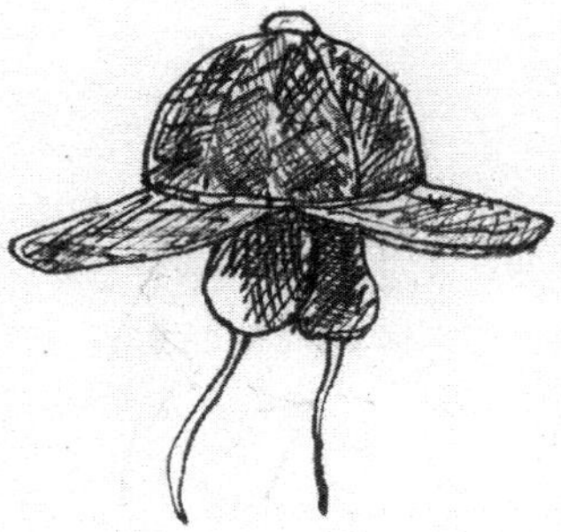

To earn a living, I wouldn't make hats or have a stall selling hats for the world. The number of people who try on hats, the funnier the better it seems, have their photograph taken, fling the hat down and then stroll off without a word of thanks seems to be on the increase.

There is a stall which sells Sherlock Holmes type deer stalkers and northern flat caps, all made out of lovely Irish tweed fabric. Dougal, an Irish boy who runs the stall, is a bit like his hats, tweedy. The Continentals in particular love to try on the Sherlock Holmes hats and no matter what their language you hear, "Sherlock Holmes" with great guffaws of laughter. Then there are the sophisticates who try on the Northern flat caps and immediately start speaking in a North Country accent, to then just fling them down on the stall without a word of thanks. To try to take advantage of the situation, I have suggested charging fifty pence a go for trying on a hat and having a photograph taken. Am I being a little unfair? Yes probably.

covered in leaves.

A portly, completely green man has just passed, his fedora hat covered in foliage and the whole of his body, including his face and hands also covered in the same green leaves. I think that he is trying to become a tree!

DANIELLA MINDER

Daniella from Colombia, who sometimes looks after my stand for me when I can't be there, had a boy friend whom she adored and they were always gazing into each other's eyes. We thought, however, it wouldn't last.

One morning, fortunately for me I came by the Market to check up on something to find her completely incapacitated, howling with tears and totally unable to set up my stall. I eventually found out between very tearful sobs that her boyfriend had dumped her – which is not a nice thing to happen to anyone. I was a bit miffed as I thought that my livelihood was as important as her being dumped but when I thought about it I had to say "not really".

We had many months of saying to her, "There's a light at the end of the tunnel, it's all for the best, he was no good anyway, you are better off without him". I do have to say my sales went down during this period but thank goodness she met someone else and is now more in love than ever and is to be married shortly. I am so pleased for her, especially as my sales have started to improve.

I casually look up from rearranging my little pictures when my eyes alight on a nice looking lady and a thin man with piercings exactly outlining his mouth. Ouch!

Chapter Twenty Three

BUSKERS

Sometimes on a Sunday I think I must be the luckiest person in the world. The closer I get to the Market, the happier I feel. Most of the stallholders feel much the same because you never know what the day may bring and there is always a buzz of excitement.

As we set up our stalls, intent also of course in hearing all the latest gossip, a wonderful operatic disembodied voice starts up. We seldom see the actual performer but the voice floats around us. I do have to say the various singers seem to have rather limited repertoires but that doesn't matter as their voices make up for it. One of the favourites is "Oh my beloved father". The acoustics are good and this blessed soprano voice reverberates round filling the air with beautiful music. We all enjoy joining in, in our own little way, feeling like would-be opera singers. It is amazing how incredibly good your own voice sounds when someone else is singing. Sometimes there is a tenor singing Nesan Dorma and we join in with that one too and no matter how many times they sing the same song, we forgive them because it is so much better than hearing the buskers blowing their whistles.

On the subject of buskers, they are an amazing bunch. This is one of the main areas in London licensed for street entertainment and they certainly make the most of it. I like the way they keep on thinking up new ideas to entertain the throngs of people finding their way through the Market but I have never managed to see any of their acts for more than a minute or so. One busker - actually a whistle-blower - asked me to draw his house. I don't often like taking on house commissions but on this occasion I was fairly interested to know what sort of place he lived in so after a little persuasion, it's no good being too eager, I agreed to do it. He said he would bring some photos in for me to work from. I was very pleasantly surprised at how very fine his house was and I did think to myself perhaps I should have a go at busking but on second thoughts no thank you. When I had finished the painting and presented it to him, another busker, a somewhat thin and scruffy character whom I had seen many times, approached me. He asked if I would like to draw either his chateau in Normandy or his little cottage in the South of France. You do get some surprises don't you? Or was he pulling my leg? I was assured that he did have these properties. I thought I must go and watch his performance and see what on earth he does, but I never did. I think they like busking because they just come up with a little idea and then they can develop it into an act and if the crowd likes it, they can then earn a very good living. In addition they have a form of control, power in a way, over their audience, rather like in pantomime and they are excellent at encouraging audience participation judging by the shouts and laughter.

There was one really odd-looking busker, a bald headed man, who bit by bit had his body tattooed all over until the whole of his head, face and body were covered. He then proceeded to have all his teeth capped in gold and not content with this he started on body piercing. He had great solid round metal earrings inserted in his earlobes rather like those African tribes you may see in films, but not as nice.

When he had succeeded in covering himself with tattoos and piercing, he then for some reason or other decided to dye himself black but you could still see vague outlines of his tattoos beneath the black dye. Every time you saw him you constantly tried to make out the tattoos under the black dye. He had a balancing act for which he wore a tartan kilt. With his thin dyed legs sticking out, it was hard to take your eyes off him when he walked by and he was quite a fascination in a morbid sort of way. Actually, when we saw him initially, we found him very scary but it turned out he was quite cultured with a nice speaking voice and apart from his appearance he seemed a decent chap. We so wanted to ask him why he was doing all this to his body, as we felt there must be some overwhelming deep reason, which we would like to know about but we rather feared all his metal teeth. Despite his appearance, I once overheard a girl, whom I can only describe as most attractive looking, asking him for a date. He agreed to this and they set a time for their liaison - you have to think there is hope for everyone but I couldn't help wondering why she did it. I wouldn't ask anyone out on a date, let alone such an odd looking individual.

Then there is "Charlie Chaplin" who is the image of his more famous name-sake. In fact if Charlie were alive today I think he would wholeheartedly approve. He comes with the cane, the black bowler hat, the walk, the feet and above all the moustache. As soon as his music comes on, we all look up and say, "Charlie's there". He seems to be very popular so perhaps I should go over and have a look but I have to earn my living and chat to my customers.

There is a tight-rope walker who dresses rather

reminiscent of a Dickens' character, a bit like Mr. Micawber. He wears a top hat, frilly shirt, tail coat and soft shoes. He ties his rope very tightly with, I suppose, one of those special scout knots between two stone pillars. When this is done to his satisfaction, he climbs up a ladder and starts to walk along the tight-rope. After reaching the other side, he then retraces his steps until he is in the centre and calmly proceeds to juggle four knives, not just three. That is quite some feat wobbling on a tight-rope without a safety net, all the time talking to amuse the crowd who by this time have congregated in great numbers. You might say, "What a way to earn your living" but the roar of the crowd and they really do roar and cheer, well that makes up for a lot.

The man with the balloon on his head is an amazing act because the performer starts off with a single upright ladder, which he places in the middle of the paved square. He wobbles a lot at first until he feels he is settled and steady. Then he gets out a latex glove and puts it over his head and proceeds to blow it up through his nose, talking all the time. How he does it I don't know! The crowd gasps every time he wobbles, whilst all the time blowing it up like a balloon until it is huge. Suddenly it bursts with a big bang, thank goodness, as you find yourself hardly able to breathe. He wipes his face and then proceeds to juggle large knives much to the amusement of the crowd. He then manages to get down from the ladder by wobbling it very wildly and jumping off to great roars from the crowd.

There is another busker who fills us with a kind of admiration. Firstly he produces a pole and asks for volunteers from the audience to hold it in place with ropes. He then places a bicycle on top of the pole, he then sits on the bicycle and juggles knives I may say to great applause.

What a spectacle it is and great fun for all!

PUNCH AND JUDY

Every year we look forward to the Punch and Judy festival which is quite amusing in so much as you can hear Punch's cackling voice echoing around the Market. We all look round and say "Oh here's Mr. Punch!" Punch and Judy shows have been performed since the 1600s and are mentioned in Samuel Pepys' diaries under entry May 9th 1662, which is now taken to be Punch's birthday. This was probably one of the first kinds of street entertainment and he is always a great draw for the children. I find it delightful to see youngsters still loving this show. Charles Dickens also mentioned Punch and Judy shows in many of his books. In the past there was a live dog, often a Jack Russell terrier, who was trained to do all kinds of things like biting Punch's nose. He had such an enormous nose, it was an obvious target for everything, including the crocodile towards the end of the show.

In earlier times, the show used to feature Punch with his big stick battering both Judy and the baby and I think he was the fore-runner of the horror movies of today. But in the end, he was always the saviour of the day, whacking everything in sight and traditionally he was the only puppet with legs. I notice that these days Punch does not whack Judy any more and quite right that is, though it is a wonder Judy doesn't whack Punch, which I suppose may be going too far but such is life!

Lovely bright Sunday, the sun is shining and everyone is in a lively mood. What a difference the weather makes. We are very weather conscious as it is essential to wear the right mix of clothes at all times. If you are either too hot or too cold it can be disastrous. I serve lots of nice Americans and Italians who seem to like buying my pictures, which is just as well as that is the main reason for me being here.

Chapter Twenty Four

ROMANCES

I would like to stress that we do work very hard as we are at the Market early in the morning and if we continue to have customers, it is often late before we close in the evening but there is still time for romance for some.

Andy Story

Andy Photos, he with the flair for organisation, was telling us that he has fallen in love with his new girlfriend, a Sikh. Now normally that would not be too much of a surprise for anyone but Andy is a devout Roman Catholic, so much so that most of his conversations are about Catholicism. He knows the bible from back to front and has always told us he could only take out Catholic girls. I may say we have had many heated discussions on this subject but they are never arguments as we like to, if possible, keep things light and convivial. This usually involves the Wednesday gang, comprising myself, Jane Ties, Harriet Scarves and Parish, these debates normally being concerned with aspects of religion. We, being creative people, like discussing the history of things and certainly we all have very lively views on all matters and that includes religions, that is until we get a bit bored with the subject or have customers to serve. Jane has had to dash off as her lovely Jewish customer has arrived hot foot from New York. He has bought from her over a hundred original ties, some bearing Jewish inscriptions as he often reads passages in Hebrew for various gatherings and likes a tie for all occasions. We often have to remind ourselves that our whole reason for being in the Market is to sell our work, earn our living, pay our mortgages and think up new creations. We are waiting with bated breath to see how Andy's romance develops.

Vyjada's Story

Vyjada, who works opposite me on Wednesdays and is from Thailand, invariably has a funny tale to tell, well unusual is probably a better word! She has a sister Misch and they have both lived in England for a long time. She makes beautiful pearl jewellery but she first started her career by making hand puppets with papier-mâché heads. These puppets were sold to shops all over the country. She told me that at one time she had received lots of love letters from her boyfriend and being very sentimental, as they were part of her past life, she didn't want to throw them away. So she kept them for quite a while until she alighted on a bright idea. Needing supplies of paper to make the puppet-heads she eventually made the decision to use these love letters for this purpose! I could hardly believe what I was hearing – why anyone should want to make papier-mâché puppet heads out of love letters I cannot imagine, but she did.

We have chuckled quite a bit over this as I thought it would come as rather a surprise if anyone should happen to look inside the head and how intriguing that might be. When you think about it, it is very ecologically minded now isn't it?

Drew's story

From time-to-time all my children have helped me out on my stall, for which I am eternally grateful and my youngest son Drew in particular showed great enthusiasm to stand in for me, although you could say the Market has always been a great place for chatting up the opposite sex, without being too obvious. I did wonder why he was frequently offering to help me but just put it down to the fact that it is an exciting place to be.

Some time ago, Kaye joined us at the Market. To be more precise she was Kaye Aromatherapy, and someone I would call a mini-star - stars like her do glow from time to time. She was a very busy lady, she mixed up all her own potions and she had even written a book on aromatherapy. Now my son loved talking to Kaye and if I arrived unannounced someone would say, "He's speaking to Kaye". It's a funny thing about attractive women like Kaye, they often seem to choose the wrong sort of man. The man she chose, we all felt, having talked about him at length and mulled it all over a great deal, was not a good influence on her. In fact it was at his insistence that she did eventually leave the Market, never to be seen again. Sorry I am digressing. Now Kaye's work was becoming more and more hectic and her massage business often took her away, so she asked friends to help her out. Lynn was invited to manage her stall at weekends in her place. So Drew's habit of enjoying a chat with Kaye now involved talking at length with Lynn. Eventually, the lovely Lynn deigned to go out with him, which was the beginning of a long love story and I am delighted to say it ended in marriage. Now all romances do not end like this. We often say, "What happened to Kaye?" as she has not been seen since nor has anyone heard from her so it does make you wonder!

Debi Tube-driver

As I mentioned, on a Wednesday I am positioned in the middle section of the Market and next to me for a number of years worked a little princess figure called Debi. I just called her that but not to her face, as she might have thought it a bit rude. The reason I thought of her in this way was because she just looked like one of Walt Disney's film princesses for instance as in "The Princess and the Pea". She had very long blond hair with a fringe and was especially petite and quite hippy-like. For years I felt she was wasted just being a minder, for that was what she was, and I felt better things were in store for her. She used to sell leather masks, not ones to wear, but to hang on the wall and she was often totally bored. The Market does have the effect on you, however, of never wanting to leave it, as there is this family feeling and should you be forced to leave, you feel as though you have been shut out. I found out that Debi had been a wonderful mother to her daughter who had needed a great deal of medical attention when she was growing up, for which I had utmost admiration. But eventually, with our encouragement, Debi decided to try to join London Underground, for which she was accepted and then she became known as Debi Tube-driver! From this point, her fortunes changed, she bought herself a house and is now married to an artist. We all take great pride in her achievements as we feel we helped her just a little to make the right decision but she is still one of the family.

Francesco's story

We have in the Market a divorce called Francesco, a rather arrogant man who thinks all women are going to swoon at his feet. I have to say some do. That's women for you, though not all women I am glad to say. He's the sort of chap who wears sun glasses in the middle of winter on a dark and gloomy day and if they are not on his nose they are on the top of his head. I

suppose, grudgingly, you could say he was quite handsome in a dark, Latin kind of way. Suddenly when a young vivacious girl arrives at the Market as a new minder we begin to notice the electricity in the air. We all exchange those knowing little looks with one another. Their gazing into each other's eyes is the great give-away but we say to ourselves, "It won't last". We know Francesco from old and it is always the same pattern because he doesn't want anything serious and the romance ends usually abruptly. Mind you, he already has three children from his marriage so he can't have much cash left, can he? Women tend to become very tearful when a romance ends but I haven't seen too many men cry over lost love affairs, but perhaps they do so over a pint of beer. Women need to be comforted with lots of platitudes and a reminder that he isn't worth crying over. My friends and I are very good in these situations, offering loads of helpful advice and acting as one big compassionate family whilst still trying to sell our goods.

Flo and Red Haired Men

Lorna Ties has a daughter Flo, who is studying at university but who also helps Lorna in the market from time to time. She has, like many others, been in and out of love quite a few times. Some little while ago, whilst helping Lorna in the Market selling her ties, she took rather a fancy to one of the young man there called Brian. She evidently has a penchant for men with red hair - yes he does have red hair. That is when he lets it grow because usually he shaves it off. He works in a family business and has a DJ career when he is not in the Market. Coming from a very musical family, his uncle is quite famous, he should do well, though it's a hard business like the arts. One has to admit it is difficult to conduct a romance at the Market as everyone is watching and can't stop talking about it a lot of the time! Brian was an honourable young man but they were not meant for one another and especially as she was in the middle of her degree course.

When the romance came to its conclusion, young Flo took solice in her studies and we all did our best to comfort her saying that it had to end sooner or later and it is never easy in any circumstances. She went back to university which pleased us all and she eventually completed her studies and was awarded a degree. At the time we were very concerned about her and hoped the break-up wouldn't affect her too much. Then lo and behold she wrote to say she had met a lovely guy living in the same accommodation building as her and guess what – he had red hair, now isn't that amazing! How quickly life changes when you are young. We know they are made for each other as they buy each other guinea pigs for presents. If one liked them and the other didn't that could be the start of problems don't you think? In fact I heard they both went into deep mourning when Princess Lally, one of their guinea pigs, died and I think Mum Lorna did her share of grieving as well.

Red-haired Brian did not appear to have anyone in particular for ages but just lately we have noticed and it is very hard not to, being as we are in many ways similar to a very large family, that he has taken an interest in Bee, who was working in the Market, but she is a most attractive girl with a huge mane of blond golden hair and lots of boyfriends so we did not think he stood a chance. We are avidly watching with bated breath. I have to report all seems to be going well on the romance front. In fact they seem to be very close except that Bee has announced that she is going to return permanently to the Czech Republic. We will be very sorry to see her go as she has been such an asset to the Market so who knows what will happen. All her family is in the Czech Republic so it is only natural that she should want to be with them. Love can be so transient, perhaps just as well.

Karrie's story

Lately Karrie has had a big romance and I must say I

do enjoy all the excitement and highs and lows. She heard by chance from her first boy-friend, who she went out with when she was fifteen years old. Now that was over thirty years ago when they were at co-educational boarding school together. It was rather like a case of "friends reunited". After a great deal of wondering whether meeting up again was a good idea, she decided to go ahead. She did worry that it might be quite embarrassing - just imagine if she didn't like the look of him and even worse if he didn't like the look of her. Thinking to herself as she did, I must be looking old or I'm too fat, would be such a dent in her confidence.

She eventually arranged to meet him on one of the bridges over the River Thames and this was a very exciting prospect but being Karrie, she went to the wrong bridge. I do understand creative people, I feel so at home with them. After much telephoning, thank goodness for mobile phones, she assured him she hadn't done it on purpose and made her way to meet him. When she eventually found him, after this gap of over thirty years, she put in a set of false party teeth and gave him a big smile. When she told me, I did give a little gasp and asked her why on earth she had done such a thing but I suppose there is just no answer to that, other than it broke the ice! Actually this is probably the best thing that has happened to her in a long time despite it being a new learning curve for her.

Chapter Twenty Five

WEDDINGS

Now I love weddings, we do have a few and they are always so unconventional, which is probably why I find them so interesting. Harry the Jeweller married his partner of twenty five years, his grown up children were in attendance, he wore a white suit he bought in Vietnam together with his open-toed sandals. I'm beginning think he must suffer from hot feet, always exposing his toes to the elements. Everyone thought Anna looked lovely and they did notice Harry's toes!

Tamara's Wedding

Tamara Wax has just married Robert Clocks. What a combination – wax and clocks! Robert is a designed of clocks which are totally original, both visually and in their mechanics and certainly intriguing. Their romance has been most interesting. I first began to wonder when Robert decided to come Salsa dancing with us, particularly as he didn't seem to want to learn. He didn't dance the entire evening but kept saying how very graceful Tamara was with her dancing and I naturally agreed with him. However, when he kept repeating how graceful and beautiful she was throughout the evening, I was beginning to get a bit bored and then I thought to myself, "Ho! ho! Must keep my eye on this". They did keep the romance all rather quiet but in due course Tamara had to return to her native Romania as her visa had run out. When

Romania joined the European Community, she was able to return and the rest is history for the pair of them.

What a lovely warm day they chose for the wedding; the ceremony was held in the Romanian church, St. Dunstan's in Fleet Street. Most of us from the Wednesday group had not been to a Romanian wedding so it was something quite different. All Tamara's family were there from Romania. The bride, of course, brought tears to our eyes as she looked so beautiful and Robert was so handsome. They had ancient silver crowns placed on their heads and they then had to circle hand in hand with the priest, three times round a table. When the ceremony was over the gates were opened in Lincoln's Inn so we could enjoy Pimms on the lawn.

The reception was held in The Old Hall, which is one of the finest buildings in London. The records tell us it was built in 1485, being erected before Christopher Columbus set sail for the New World. It was regularly used for sittings of the Court of Chancery and indeed the famous opening scene of Dickens' "Bleak House" was set there. The wooden screen designed by Inigo Jones at the South End and Hogarth's painting of "Paul before Felix" made us all feel very grand.

The meal was exceptional, the drinks flowed freely and the ambiance both Romanian and English passed all expectations. We danced till dawn and thought ourselves very fortunate to have been invited to such a happy occasion. We even joined in Romanian dancing which was very fast and we now know why they all keep so slim.

Of course some of our party became a little inebriated but that just added to the fun.

MALE MENOPAUSE

Pierre , one of our traders, is sporting a new hairstyle. He must be about fifty and has just returned from holiday. To our amazement he has dyed his hair a shade of auburn, shaved the sides leaving it rather tufty on the top and back. Mind you as long as he feels good, who are we to comment? He does look slightly reminiscent of a curly hedgehog with shaved sideburns.

STRANGE SUBSTANCES

The people who work alongside you do become your friends, even though you may not be too sure of them in the first place. The man next to me, a curious character who is leaving today, who I have not been next to before, makes silver bracelets He has actually been asked to leave as he spends more time drinking instead of working. He has just told me he is going to start up on his own making jewellery which I feel might be a good thing and give him some sort of direction in his life. It's quite a demanding job as there are so many jewellers it requires quite a lot of talking in order to get good sales. As he was standing next to me, you cannot help but chat since you just can't stop yourself as you have the whole day in front of you. He does look a little worse for wear, rather like a scarecrow, if you know what I mean but even between conversations we had, he did work hard selling the bracelets and rings. I do not know how we came to be discussing drugs but we did. I have to confess that I abhor drugs of any kind, I certainly hate even taking aspirin. I don't think he was trying to impress me but he told me about all the things he had taken and the last one was horse anaesthetic! I had great difficulty in keeping the horror off my face but he then told me it had nearly blown his head off. Every time I looked at him I thought he must think he's a horse, only kidding, but I couldn't wait to tell my friends about it. Mind you I find it very interesting hearing about what people get up to but I don't think I now could have him as a friend.

The fashion this winter is to wear very short shorts over thick black tights - I think it's just an excuse to show off your legs!

On Saturdays I am wedged between Anne Bears and her teddy bears and Harry the Jeweller. Now I think Anne Bears has got an admirer though she certainly doesn't need anyone else as she has a very nice partner Peter, and a granddaughter who lives with her to keep her occupied, as well as the constant making of teddy bears. Each

Saturday he arrives and insists on buying us coffee and cake and even if we don't want it we accept, as it would be rather churlish of us to refuse. He is always very helpful to Anne in demonstrating her teddy bears. We have to ask him what he has been doing in order to be polite and then he starts. He sometimes says he has been working undercover to track down Russian insurgents. He also tells us that he has been down on the Kings Road as an undercover detective for MI5 trying to ferret out would-be assassins. We of course take it all with a pinch of salt and when he has disappeared, he never overstays his welcome, we just roll our eyes! I suppose you could say he is reliving his dreams as what man doesn't want to be an MI5 agent? Every week we get a different story from him. We have heard he works in a shop selling luggage – but who knows?

Chapter Twenty Six

STATUES

As you walk along the streets near the Market, you will come across men and women who transform themselves into living statues forming a part of the ongoing entertainment which surrounds the Market. This sort of attraction has been going on for centuries in this part of London and I am sure will continue to do so for many - ears to come. I still get the feeling of seeing Eliza Doolittle scurrying along. The "statue" people all have their own ideas as to how to attract attention and in the course of doing so make money. We frequently see a man who looks as though he is running in the wind and somehow he makes his shirt and coat look as though they are caught by the breeze and in particular his tie is sticking right out at an angle.

Another "statue" is painted almost completely silver, wearing silver clothing and standing like a Roman Centurion. He is a fine figure of a man, I would think a body builder. How he can remain motionless for so long is a mystery to me. You can see similar "statues" in many cities but the ones around the Market are excellent. The Centurion has recently been head-hunted for the Royal Opera House and has taken part in one of their operas to great acclaim.

One that always intrigues me is the man without a head. He has a chair with a high back to it and he sits there with a space where his head should be. It is obvious his head is hidden in his jacket but there he sits with his hat and spectacles suspended above where his head should be, rather like the invisible man. It is very eye-catching and you continually find yourself wondering how he has actually hidden his head. I can't imagine just how boring it must be sitting there motionless for such a long period of time.

Jane Ties said, "You must take a look at the man who pretends to be a dog". He is a giggle, no matter how many times we have seen him. He has a large wooden box, which somehow he fits into, and on top of the box is placed a small kennel. In front of this are a pair of brown hairy paws and at the back there is a brown hairy tail which wags. When you look into the kennel, you see the man's face, which he has painted to resemble a dog with a little black nose and small black dots round his mouth for whiskers and a brown patch round one of his eyes. He attracts the attention of the passers-by making dog-like noises, then spouting off on topical subjects for instance the Mayor of London, intermittently creating a very lively conversation with anyone who cares to converse with him. His animated face will certainly enliven anyone who takes time to stop and look and it is almost impossible not to laugh, so much so I think it would amuse even the most depressed person. One does wonder how they think up these ingenious ideas.

It always seems to me a pretty hard way to earn a living but again it is all about entertainment and the “statues” seem to revel in the adulation from the crowds, especially the children.

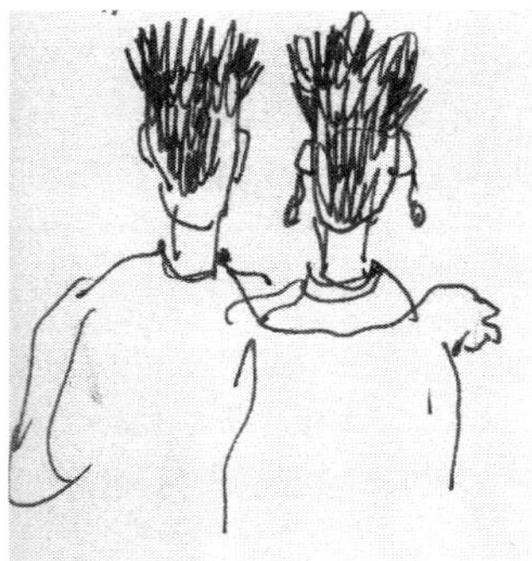

A grey haired couple pass by with exactly the same haircuts, short back and sides, spikes up on top, rather reminiscent of a pair of hedgehogs.

MAN WITH THE FERRETS

Here he comes again, the man with the ferrets, we wonder to ourselves where does he get them from. He has two ferrets in the hood of his anorak and that’s how he carries them. They are on leads but they seem very happy and contented where they are with their little noses peeping out from time to time. He told us he was taking them to the park for their daily walk. We felt we would like to know a bit more about him as it is not every day you come across such a character.

It turns out that he has quite a menagerie at home comprising another albino ferret, which someone had left on his doorstep, a raccoon, a kitten, a parrot, a lizard and a snake. Now I don't believe this is possible but he says he takes the snake out for a walk but only on very warm days. On closer questioning we found out he wraps it round his neck and he then walks round the park. That sounds more like it. Now his lizard, which is quite large, he does have on a lead and he takes it also along to the park for a walk - this we will definitely have to see! Perhaps on second thoughts we won't. He said that he has rescued all the animals and by looking at his photographs, they are beautifully looked after. I did think he smelt a bit "zooish", however, but we felt he was such a nice man and we couldn't help believe everything he said! He certainly attracts attention, as you can imagine all the people passing by him either jump back in horror or are absolutely fascinated. We always keep well away as ferrets, so we have been told, bite and then won't let go. I wouldn't like the embarrassment of serving customers with a ferret attached to my finger.

One Sunday, I was early at work and intent on discussing with the others some new rule that had been imposed on our free spirits when Karrie dashed over saying, "Have you heard the latest?" She then recounted the story of what had happened to one of the minders the previous evening before she left work. She decided she would fetch herself a coffee. Now at that time we had an

Italian restaurant nearby supplying us with refreshments all day and every day, so we got to know the staff quite well. There is a door on either side and we usually go in one way and out the other. This particular evening both doors appeared to be shut and the restaurant was in darkness as though closed. One of the Market girls, however, said that she had seen a small light on in the restaurant and decided to give the door a try. To her astonishment when peering in on entering, she caught sight of Aldo, one of the waiters, in flagrante delicto against the ice cream cabinet. She let out a piercing scream which took him entirely by surprise and she leapt out of the other door like a bat out of hell. We found this story absolutely mind-boggling but did feel sorry for Aldo. He was never to be seen again, completely disappeared from the face of the earth. The girl found our amusement a trifle annoying as she said it was not amusing to her at the time. I agreed with her and I said furthermore I could never fancy anything from the ice cream cabinet again. After that the jokes did become somewhat ribald and the story kept us amused for quite a time. Sorry to say we have now lost our coffee shop as the restaurant is gone, replaced by a clothes shop and so far not half as funny.

A very strange moustache has just floated by. The bowler-hatted owner had a moustache so long that he was able to curl it round into two complete circles which reached out either side of his chubby red face. We felt he must have used gel or maybe super glue as they were completely rigid as he

walked along.

Chapter Twenty Seven

THEM AND US (Part 2)

The last Market Manager as I mentioned was a disaster for us because she was heavily influenced by two "bought-ins" (those standholders who are not craftsmen) so that the quality of the merchandise went completely unchecked. We have often mulled over this unholy alliance and how they managed to exert such control over us. We felt quite helpless at times as we had no-one to air our views to. This situation continued only to the benefit of the "bought-ins" and not to the craftsmen. To be fair she was following an agenda set by the owners of the Market to make as much money as possible to help any future re-sale value. If you are a craftsman you love your work and take great pride in your workmanship and creativity so it is difficult to accept people who just go along to wholesalers and buy goods "Made in China" and then profess they have been up all night making them. We wouldn't mind if they didn't tell lies and just admitted they were playing the system. But we always try hard to be pleasant and friendly to them whilst underneath we do feel a great deal of animosity. We had to concur with everything they did as to get on the wrong side of them would be to the detriment of our own businesses.

The situation continued for a long time and then suddenly, out of the blue, everything has now changed. The Market has been bought out by a very large international company, whose intent is to alter everything. We were all enthusiastic as we felt we needed change. We had hoped that things would be for the better in as much as we would lose all the bought-in goods and that we would get a fair deal but now we are beginning to wonder. We have seen the Market change hands many times so we will just wait and see. We believe we are all going to be branded, as far as we can tell, that is conforming to an agenda which as yet we are not privy to.

The talk at the moment is that shortly management are having a meeting to discuss who is going to be invited to stay at the Market and who will be going and to clarify who are the "bought-ins". We are evidently to be categorized as A, B or C. We are all waiting with bated breath as to the outcome.

We understand that interviews are going to be held to determine whether category Cs should be re-graded, which could be most complicated. A Wednesday jeweller, Judo black belt and civil engineer, who now sells his own designer jewellery, has been called for an interview. He considered whether he should walk in wearing Saffron robes with hands in prayer fashion and scatter holy water from the Ganges, hopefully splashing onto their good suits. We all thought it might be fun if everyone else dressed up and held their hands in prayer but not everyone agreed to this and thought it might be a bit risky.

Generally, on Sundays when Karrie is off, I have an assortment of different nationalities working alongside me. Last week it was a very charming girl who came from Istanbul and is here to perfect her English. Her spoken English is excellent but sometimes it takes a little while before she understands exactly what you mean. A young girl, dressed in black, passed by with her boyfriend and she had the longest false eye lashes you have ever seen, looking a little ridiculous. I drew her attention to this aspect of the girl's appearance but she could not understand the word "eyelashes" and by the time I had managed to explain, the moment had passed!

Chapter Twenty Eight

WINTER

When Winter comes, it is vital for us to follow the weather forecasts as it is essential to have the right clothes on you at all times. In fact the colder it becomes the more the conversation centres around keeping warm. Great discussions take place as to the best and cheapest thermal underwear. You will find that the trendiest of young girls and even men delight in finding the warmest tights and long johns which they would normally think of with disgust as being old fashioned and definitely not "with-it".

The Market was originally set up where it is today because of the prevailing cool winds blowing through, which kept the produce fresh in summer. In the days before refrigeration, it was necessary to have these fresh breezes with their cooling effect. In Summer the breeze is very welcome but in winter there is an especially strong wind chill factor, which we know only too well. The Market is covered overhead but open at each end and when the wind whistles through it can become quite alarmingly cold.

Over time, we have evolved special ways of keeping ourselves warm yet looking quite reasonable as we don't want to put the customers off too much by looking like the Yeti. Standards again! One topic of conversation is how many layers you have managed to put on without actually falling over - mind you I'm sure we would all bounce straight back up! I remember Martin Flowers telling me, then showing me, that he had seven tee shirts on, not that I wanted to see anyway. I find it is best to wear either thin layers of cotton or Kashmir wool. Kashmir is expensive but it is very light and extremely warm.

I have noticed that the head-ware which makes an appearance in Winter is becoming more and more extreme, year after year. At one time men would only wear conventional hats whereas women have always been a bit more adventurous. Now I have the vision before me of one of the jewellers wearing a strange woolly fair aisle, pointy, knitted hat with plaits for ties which makes me think of him as tribesman coming down from the mountains of Bolivia on his donkey. He is not the only one as it seems to be the latest fashion - I suppose all that matters is keeping warm!

Amazingly, even on the most bitterly cold Winter days we still have customers who come to support us. You might think why on earth do we all choose to withstand the elements like this but I have to say that it is the camaraderie which draws us here and the money as we have to live don't we? If we don't work we don't earn any money.

The months running up to Christmas are very important to all of us who work in the Market as it can be a make or break time for many traders. We have to decide on which new designs we are going to promote and we usually start work in September trying to get our ideas into production.

Jane and Lorna's ties take on a new festive aspect and

Karrie's cards become more extravagant by the minute. Often they now have lights and musical boxes incorporated in them one way or another. I have found that special Christmas pictures are popular, something you can bring out with the Christmas decorations or give as a present. After all it is said a picture is a joy for ever.

All the jewellers really polish up their best pieces, always have them beautifully displayed and sparkling under the lights. The polishing never stops. Jewellery is definitely a Christmas item. Darell, one of the jewellers, has a splendid array of his own designs on show. He is really the top jeweller in the Market having made jewellery for many of the most prestigious London stores and he even devises his own special clasps. What a craftsman! He is now on the panel for judging crafts and we all have a lot of faith in him.

Chapter Twenty Nine

ANNABEL POEMS

Annabel Poems is about forty, a successful poet who has written many poems, which she has had published. She looks rather austere as she wears round metal rimmed spectacles which give her an owl-like stare probably because the glasses magnify her eyes. We all think she is very intellectual as she makes up crossword puzzles and even devises her own cryptic crosswords. She tends to give the appearance of being a little old maidish, if I dare say this in these politically correct times. Not only is she constantly working on a new poem but she is also an avid knitter. This added to the whole look, rather like the women knitting at the time of the French Revolution but she didn't knit names into her garments, thank goodness. Sometimes you were left wondering what on earth she was knitting in grey and black wools, when it turned out to be a bat! I supposed someone would buy it. She did knit other things such as mice, frogs, bees and cats together with an assortment of other items. Then everyone in the Market began to collect them, especially the bees and we still have them.

One year Adrian, who organises our outings, decided to arrange a special party for us in a night club in Soho and he suggested that if anyone wanted to entertain us, they should let him know. Now Annabel offered to recite the poem "Arthur and the Lion". When her turn came we all felt a bit embarrassed for her and started looking at one another thinking this is not going to be fun. She looked rather hot and red faced as she wearing her hand knitted mohair dress. She started to recite the words and suddenly her complete persona changed and we saw a very different Annabel. She became full of life, very animated and made us all laugh so much that we could hardly believe it was the same person. We realized that under this owl-like exterior was a very funny and passionate woman. We were quite spell-bound and gave her a standing ovation with everyone wanting more. After that she became quite a celebrity with everyone asking where and when her next recital would be held. She told us she would be reciting a poem about teeth and was going to wear a hat shaped like a tooth. "Oh!, we said, "That sounds nice".

Annabel was followed by another of our band of players, Ruth the Pilot. I always think of her as being like a Russian doll, each layer reveals a new person. She is a qualified pilot, rides a motorbike, makes and sells her own jewellery and does belly dancing but to look at her slight figure and calm air you would never think she was so outgoing. Whenever we have an outing she arrives on her motor bike, clad in skin tight leathers, which always comes as a surprise having such a quiet persona. She announced she would entertain us with a belly dance, which we felt was an exciting prospect. She often performs at corporate functions so we thought she would be very professional and she was. Her costume was most authentic, with lots of little bells, sequins, tassels and with her perfect body and long gleaming dark hair swirling around her, little bells tinkling as she moved, she gave an outstanding performance which was heartily appreciated by everyone. What talent we have in our midst!

The next act was Rachel with her long red hair. She

teaches modern dance when not working in the Market. Her dance was like a modern ballet with a strong theatrical air about it, lots of leaping and twirling to lovely music, completely free and again this was very exotic and much appreciated by us all. This act was followed by two of the girls giving a Salsa demonstration. They had obviously put in a lot of practice as they seemed to us to be most proficient. Two of the boys, Pip and Mo, sons of Martin Flowers, gave a very good rap performance as well as DJ'ing for the night, which is what they do for a living. I have forgotten to mention that the compere for the night was Brendan Teeshirts and he amused us very much as he was dressed in drag which was a little out of character for him in his normal life. Well you never know! By now the entertainment had gone on for quite some considerable time so we felt it was time for dancing and with that everyone jumped to their feet and let off steam.

Annabel did have a little secret, although she tried very hard to hide it but we could not help noticing something, as we are quite observant on the whole, to put it mildly. The object of her affection was fellow stallholder Tim, who was married with some children, although somewhat unhappily I think. He never actually said so but we just got that impression as he always seemed a little brow-beaten. As he lived out of town he was always late for work and had to leave early to catch his train so Annabel willingly set up his stall and closed it for him. Now that clinched it for us, it must be infatuation. No-one would do that for just an ordinary friend now would they? It's such jolly hard work. We never really knew if Tim liked her or not, as I have mentioned before, men don't like to discuss these sort of things and particularly with us in the Market. If she hadn't have looked so prim and proper we probably wouldn't have commented upon it but it did become a great topic of conversation and interest as to what was actually going on. Tim was a rather handsome sort of chap and really a nice man.

In the end the whole situation changed because Tim wasn't making enough money and decided to leave the market, which does happen from time to time. I have noticed with great interest how some people seem to have a non-stop business, then suddenly it just falls away. I suppose the answer is to always try and keep changing even if it is only slightly and introduce new ideas. No matter how much you enjoy the life it cannot be sustained if you are not selling and it then becomes a burden. We did hear that he had got divorced and had become a teacher. After that Annabel also left and we heard she went to live near an old beau from her youth. We still think fondly of her.

Chapter Thirty

HALLOWEEN

I don't get much excited about Halloween as witches don't figure too heavily in my repertoire of images and I think that goes for the other traders as well. We were somewhat intrigued when suddenly to our astonishment large pumpkins appeared on the Piazza grouped together and when I say large, enormous would be a better word. They were so big that it was almost impossible to see over them. We all wondered, of course, where they had come them from, most probably from an outsize vegetable shop! Luckily they remained intact as, having a rather vivid imagination, I could imagine what could happen if they became over ripe.

CHERRY MINDER

Cherry has just returned from a three week trip to Thailand so we have been waiting with some anticipation to see some of the outfits she has brought back. She arrived today in a medley of pale mint green and pistachio, her hair has been tinted with purple streaks so perhaps she is in a purple phase. She was wearing a sort of headdress, well I think you may well call it that, but it consisted of several flimsy silk scarves wound round her head with a large lilac flower sticking out at the side. In her ears were enormous dangling earrings, round her neck a long necklace made from various baubles, lilac and green in colour, ending with a nine inch pale green heart made of wood. Hanging below the necklace, she had a huge pearl shell threaded onto green ribbon. She wore several layers of silky green and lilac fabric with lace intertwined all of different lengths, finished off by a pair of long haired Yeti boots in pale lilac. It was a cold day so she did need warm boots! She told us that she had travelled from Thailand in the same outfit - on the aeroplane they may have taken her for foreign royalty or a film star, who knows.

Birdie Boots. A pair of birdie boots walked past – they were in bright purple suede, knee length and the feet were fashioned rather resembling a bird's foot. I suppose they were very comfortable.

Chapter Thirty One

CHRISTMAS TIME

The months leading up to Christmas are, as I have said, very important to us all, as this is one of the major purchasing times of our year. Normally a huge Christmas tree adorns the Piazza and one year to everyone's dismay it fell down, caused by the high wind I think. At one time there was a grotto with Father Christmas for the children, a huge decorated fir tree and mulled wine on sale, all helping to make a very festive spirit pervading throughout the Market and this was our traditional Christmas which carried on this way for many years. Customers came from all over the world to soak up this wonderful atmosphere and especially the children's grotto. This year with the new management, it was decided to have a very modern approach at huge cost with all the decorations in white with little "pea lights" as they are called with magenta, blue and pink flood lights shining through them. Instead of the traditional tree, there was a large white laser tree beautifully projected on to the side of St. Paul's Church and I felt it was quite magical, rather like being on the set of Narnia. In some ways it did give that frosty feeling which you associate with Christmas but on the other hand tended to give a gloomy atmosphere, especially as it gets dark so early in December. We decided we would have preferred a more traditional Christmas.

However, we did enjoy some amazing new entertainers. One act entailed a huge helium balloon with a lady ballerina floating underneath - I suppose you could call it aerobatics. The balloon was lit with soft laser lights which, as darkness came, created a luminous atmosphere like a huge moon floating around. If invited, we would have all quite happily had a go, floating about and ridding us I'm sure of our pre-Christmas stress.

Another incredible act comprised four large balls on poles which were beautifully lit with laser beams in purple, magenta, red, green and blue creating intensely beautiful combinations of different colours and then much to everyone's amazement, out popped four little people dressed in white. They really were little, not dwarfs, as someone saw them on the ground and said they were just very petite - well you wouldn't fit a large person in would you! They proceeded to swing very wildly from side to side, catching each other's hands and bowing one way and then the other rather like an aeriel ballet dance with again these wonderful colours making extraordinary patterns of light. It was a wonderful spectacle of form and colour.

There was very strict security while all this was going on, as you can imagine youngsters wanting to climb the poles and join in but they didn't. We did enjoy our mulled wine though, which helped to keep out the evening chill.

We all had to turn round and look at a group of girls, well not quite girls, a little older perhaps. We think they were dressed for going out on the town not for a fancy dress party! One in particular with a big blond hair-style took our attention as she was rather well endowed in every possible way and was sporting a very short purple and black tutu so that we all visibly gasped. I think perhaps it was the added sight of very sturdy legs in high heeled boots that did it.

One of the Market traders, in fact almost one of the originals, always has a hat or scarf on his head. It is never anything outrageous but quite insignificant with his long hair sticking out from underneath it. He has never been seen without his head covered, so we wonder if perhaps he is completely bald except for the hair sticking out round the edge rather like a flue brush. We have even said we would contribute to a major charity if he would let us see what is under his hat – but he won't. Perhaps a gale force wind might do the trick.

Annie, who is a minder and works for a jeweller, is a really incredibly compassionate person and I would have to add that most people in the Market are. She came to tell us she had seen a man, a vagrant, lying on the floor and that he had been horribly sick. Everyone was walking past him – I wouldn't think badly of anyone who does walk past as these people can be very scary and have been known to jump up and stab you. I gave her a bottle of water for him as I was in the middle of serving a customer and she went back to give him some help. She was so concerned that in the end she sent for an ambulance which came promptly and took him to hospital.

We of course discuss occurrences such as this and Dasha, from the Czech Republic who makes exquisite baby clothes, said that in her country there was no such thing as the welfare state and it amazes her how some people end up this way when there is so much help available and life is so much easier. She says if you do not work in her country, you will starve and it makes you take more care of yourself even if you have an addiction. The other way of thinking about it is that they just die and that is that.

At one time we had in the Market a very nice trader

called Wallace, who looked a picture of health and well-being. He used to help his partner Alicia with her enamel jewellery and we saw quite a lot of him. He eventually told us he had been a "down-and-out" in London, sleeping rough in doorways - we could hardly believe him. His story began to unfold and he told us he had at one time had his own business but unfortunately it had failed. At this point his wife left him taking with her their children and he then dissolved into being an alcoholic, sleeping rough where ever he could. It was Alicia, who rescued him and became his new partner and encouraged him back into the mainstream of life for which he is everlastingly grateful. Unfortunately the damage done by leading such a life does leave its mark and he bravely fought cancer for many years. It always seems so sad that the past has to catch up with one in such a devastating way.

I sometimes wonder about girls or for that matter men who grow their hair so long that it nearly reaches the ground and they are almost able to stand on it - it seems to be a bit of a fetish. We all turned round to have a look at a girl who has such long hair that it could probably trip her up. I think it is because we all have to take a look which creates the obsession with their hair because if no one looked, or commented, what would be the point?

Chapter Thirty Two

CHRISTMAS PARTY

As it is Christmas-time we decided we must have a party. We like parties as much as we do outings. On a Saturday, I work next to Feisty Caroline, she does have a fiery temper at times but I must admit she can arrange a very good party. To be fair she does have an overwhelming number of good qualities and who am I to judge! I am not that perfect myself now am I? When it comes to organising parties, she goes to great lengths to get everything right, it's the creativeness again. It was decided that we should hold it in a nightclub near to the Market. We have our parties on a Sunday if possible as Monday is of course our day off. A fancy dress party was the theme as everyone likes dressing up. Great discussions were going on as to what we should all wear. Everyone thinks I should be good at designing outfits but I am not - I'm just a painter, I'm afraid.

There was great excitement as the party drew near. Those who said they would be too tired to go were persuaded that they would enjoy it and could surely make up an outfit. I had decided I would go as the spy Mata Hari, as I had in my wardrobe just the right black dress, a cigarette holder and one of those imitation cigarettes which actually smokes when you puff it.

The party was a great success. Someone, however, did remark that I had worn the same outfit to the last fancy dress party we had but I felt sure no one would have remembered.

When we arrived at the night club we were greeted by Madame Pompadour, who is in fact a very attractive Turkish girl and had hired this exquisite outfit for the night so she really did look the part. Next came Caroline, I think she was the Mad Hatter and quite apt I thought with top hat and tails along with her partner who came as a surgeon. Little Bee – we can never pronounce her name as she comes from the Czech Republic, so we just call her Bee which luckily she doesn't mind - came as a red devil. She was wearing a short red PVC tunic with red PVC knee-length boots, red horns carrying a devil's prong, I think you would call it. Thankfully, she didn't use it. Among other party-goers was a selection of fairies and doctors and Dracula with a particularly active cape, actually making a bit of a nuisance of himself, floating about and trying to bite people when they weren't looking. After the first few times it got a bit tiresome. Chris, a nice Polish boy came as another surgeon and it was not until the end of the evening that I realized who he was - I think it was the mock blood all over his coat and even on his hat and face that put me off getting too close.

Three Arabs arrived in wonderful robes, moustaches and headgear and their attire and make-up was so good I still don't know who they were. Having just come back from Dubai, I really thought they might have been authentic. The wonderful thing about our parties is that as soon as the music begins everyone jumps up and dances - it's having so many free spirits all being together that does it. The dancing gets wilder and wilder as the evening progresses. I suppose it's the bubbles helping again. I did notice there were quite a few schoolgirls with satchels who were dancing in rather a grown up fashion, one of which was Jael. When you live where I do out in the country everyone is more sedate and you have to wait until you are asked to dance and then it becomes all very orderly. There is very little wild dancing as everyone would stare at you and think you are rather silly.

There were prizes awarded for the best fancy dress costume and first prize went to a small bald man in a dark suit who had two horns attached to his head, by suction I think. We didn't think he had done enough to be awarded first prize but someone else must have. Darling Tilly, Karrie's daughter, came as a traditional Russian doll with bright red cheeks and big eyelashes painted on, wearing a typical Russian style peasant dress, Cossack fur hat and black shiny boots. We all thought she deserved to have been the winner.

As I had been dancing for about four hours in very high heeled boots, by midnight my feet felt we should leave, that is myself and my long-suffering husband. He is quite happy as long as I find an attractive friend to sit with him which in this instance was New Zealand born Jo, who is a tall beautiful blonde, the wife of Dracula, he with the cape. I believe the party went on until the wee small hours with a lot of shenanigans going on, so I'm told. Several people went for a Champagne breakfast afterwards but this would have been too much for me.

A man in a hat with long ears rather like a basset hound passes by. Men and their hats again, they are getting more and more daring. Each finger on his hand had a long claw-like silver ring. It is Chinese New Year so perhaps that has something to do with it.

Chapter Thirty Three

THEM AND US (Part 3)

On the dreaded Thursday, the first of the fourteen interviews were held and these lasted continuously from eleven in the morning until five o'clock with a six man board of management. Everyone came out rather shaken as it was a pretty searching session and all had been asked to prove that their merchandise was their own. We all agree that this is necessary for the future quality of the Market but actually it should be obvious. I can certainly tell, and so can any other craftsperson what has been made by hand or bought from a wholesaler. It appears that we shall all have to be interviewed, this being the first time in my life that I have been asked to prove I am the originator of my art work. It seems like taking a sledge hammer to crack a nut. We are just hoping all the artisans get through.

One such artisan, who makes bracelets from silver and is quite a character on the Market, was also classified as category C and we were much amused by his account of the interview. He and his partner had started off with a great strategy to psych themselves up and go together as a forceful team. The meeting room was on the fourth floor and unfortunately they hadn't realized there was a lift as it was so well hidden, so by the time they got there they were out of breath and it completely took the wind out of

their sails. But even so, they did manage to start their interview as in television's "Dragons Den" with the spokesman saying, "We will give you ten per cent of the company for £100,000". Can you imagine the faces of the panel? There was incredulity, astonishment, disbelief and then the interviewing panel did laugh but I don't think uproariously. We ourselves could not stop chortling at the description of their faces and we thought he was truly brave and fearless. This is one of the strengths of the Market traders, whatever the situation, as it has been lately with the new management, they can always resort to laughter. We have since heard that they have been up-graded to category B and when we heard the good news, we all gave a cheer.
The next round of interviews of category Cs is now due.

One of the Wednesday jewellers, initially heard that he had not been re-graded. I wonder whether he should have sprinkled the water from the Ganges after all. We were rather annoyed at this decision as his jewellery is very unusual. He has most attractive designs and we thought he had been unfairly treated as having a family to support, things would be very difficult for him. But I am glad to say he has now been reassessed and upgraded to category B, so what was all the fuss about I have to ask myself? There are many others in the same situation and hoping for an upgrade. The whole procedure has become very stressful and we all think that it could have been handled over a month not a year and everyone would have been less anxious as to their future.

It's always the hair that does it.

Karrie's life is one of complete highs and lows in the extreme. One Sunday, when she arrived at the Market, she told us that after work on Thursday she had gone to do some shopping and fainted outside a well known departmental store. A passer-by promptly called the emergency services but with all the fuss and bother getting her into the ambulance, someone stole her purse. It is hard to believe that anyone can do such a thing. The hospital wanted to admit her but she insisted on going home. Then out of the blue during the course of the next day she received a huge order for cards from the sister of the King of Saudi Arabia. Invitations for a wedding she told me.

A nod from Lorna.

Rod Stewart walked past, not really him, it was just a look-alike but he had all the right mannerisms. Must be in a show. It did make you look twice.

Whenever I walk through the narrow cobbled streets that lead to the Market, seeing with people dashing about their business or watching the entertainers, it fills me with a great sense of history. Ordinary English people have been coming here to buy and be entertained for centuries. The stallholders have always been there to sell their goods, make a living and to be also entertained by the customers because it works both ways. You do have a sense of déjà vu. From the days when it was a convent garden, it has slowly grown throughout the years. With attractive town houses lining the streets around the church, the area started evolving to what it is today. St Paul's Church is on one side of the Piazza and both are designed by Inigo Jones. The tall buildings which surround it were the homes of rich merchants from the past. Perhaps they too traded in fruit and veg who knows? The area has had quite a chequered history and has become run down from time to time but then its fortunes have changed with wealthy landowners moving in.

CHANGING FASHIONS

A young girl passes by wearing
a navy and white striped head
band, tied at the back. She has
a white jacket with very large
black polka dots and
underneath she has on a
tomato coloured dress teamed
with bright blue mesh tights
and red and white polka dot
shoes. She comes complete
with blond spiky hair and an
attitude to suit.

Chapter Thirty Four

WIZARDS

We once had a Wizard in our midst. A dear friend of us all who was into mystical occurrences enrolled on a wizardry course. Karrie and I were a little sceptical as to how you could learn to be a wizard but evidently you can become one by taking special wizardry lessons. After a period of serious study you become a baby wizard but this still does not allow you to cast any spells, even if they are beneficial ones. We did ask what sort of spells you would be able to do if you graduated to be a full wizard and the reply was that you could turn water into wine, so we thought that was a very good thing to do. After about six months of hard study, our friend became a wizard. I requested she put a spell on all my pictures so that they would sell faster than usual but this never happened! Sadly our dear wizard friend died recently and we still miss her, with her creative mind and her unusual look at life but her aura remains with us.

Have just been to see a quartet playing classical music. The sound of their music kept drifting through so I asked my friends to mind my stall whilst I went to have a look. There is nothing sweeter than violins played well.

Chapter Thirty Five

TRAVELS IN A CAMPER VAN

It was a lovely Sunday morning when Karrie arrived to greet me with her great news that she intended to buy a VW camper van. I had no idea what that was until she explained. Her daughter Tilly, who has been learning the business, would take over her stall during her search. A camper van was duly found and purchased second hand but it needed a lot of renovation. The owners had, however, loved it very much and called it Joan Mary so that meant it had a very good Karma about it which is all important to Karrie. It did require a new engine and gearbox before it was quite sound enough to be put on the road. All fittings were taken out and replaced with great skill and attention to detail. The original colour scheme was lime green and pink and was restored immaculately ending up by being quite delightful. The day before she was to depart for her travels, we all had a final look at the finished article. Everything was miniaturized with great attention to detail so that they had everything they needed without using up too much space. It was immaculate, with wicker baskets on the roof, specially treated so they would not let in the rain, which put our minds at rest. On the back were two bicycles, one with a wicker basket with flowers decorating the rim. Inside, the seating was beautifully upholstered in soft lime green leather, piped in rose pink and matching the whole colour theme were flowers lining the dash board. There were little ceramic flying birds fastened all over the walls. The sink and cooker were delightfully disguised and everything so exquisitely fitted in, quite a work of art, reminiscent of her cards. There was even a place for the computer – quite essential - we must keep in touch, which we will do?

.

The most joyous thing in life is to be able to earn your living doing something that you would do as your beloved hobby and that is how I feel about my life, very fortunate.

Chapter Thirty Six

MILITANCY

At the moment there is deep resentment in the Market because of the lack of communication. The latest to be targeted are the buskers. They feel very strongly that they are being denied their living, particularly as there have been buskers in the Market for the past four hundred years. They have already approached the London evening papers to try and get their views aired and tomorrow morning they are holding a press conference with radio, television news and major newspaper reporters. The latest rumour is that a well known opera singer has offered to give support to their cause which I think will make history. We are all waiting expectantly to see if their story actually makes the news and that it will resolve their plight. Oh, we do like a bit of excitement!

I have just seen a bed of nails going past being wheeled by a young man dressed neatly in a suit with his hair spiked up, hedgehog style with each point dyed blue. It does make you wonder whether he sits on them, stands on them or lies on them. Must look out for him and see what he does.

Update on result!

The buskers put on a wonderful show for the television cameras. The opera singers, musicians and clowns all turned out in support and it became a delightful show rather reminiscent of an old English fair. Staging their demonstration on the Piazza was banned by the management as they own the land and the security guards were out in full to keep them off. Not to be deterred, they found that they could use the land by St. Paul's which is owned by the church and there they were able to talk to the media in safety. All the Market people joined in and being a warm balmy day, it took on quite a festive air. Even the famous opera singer Lesley Garratt was there to give her support to ensure that the entertainment which has traditionally been in Covent Garden will continue. To be fair the buskers are sometimes too loud, particularly with their whistle blowing but I just feel that if they just toned it down a little everyone would be happy.

When you have a militant force determined to put their point of view across, it does make others want to join the bandwagon so we shall see what happens. It makes me think that most of the problems we have, whether it is in business, political or personal relationships, it always comes down to lack of communication and to be perceived to be treated unfairly. There are many of us who have seen it all before, in fact many times.

Life certainly is a
challenge

Chapter Thirty Seven

THEM & US - Finale

Almost all throughout its history, it seems the Market has been fighting to preserve its identity to stop it being changed too radically or its character altered irrevocably and from archaeological evidence, they say the Market is the oldest inhabited part of London. It's the people who have lived nearby, together with the ordinary traders, with the help of the Trust who have managed, very often by the skin of their teeth, to preserve it. All too often in the recent past it has been a close run thing. It's when Big Business thinks it is going to steam-roller through changes, and make us into a brand, which would alter the whole concept and ambience of the place that the little people band together to try and stop the onward race to completely change everything so that the past is totally forgotten. We feel there are quite enough retail malls and departmental stores and accept that though everyone naturally wants to make improvements, they should not totally destroy the surroundings so that they will be lost for ever. We just hope we can all have some input as to how changes can be made without destroying the free atmosphere and the creative liveliness that is the Market.

We are now feeling that perhaps the Market might be

returning to what it was intended, which is a market for original craftsmen to sell their original wares.

Much to my amazement I have been awarded a category A grade which was so exciting that I had to go out and have a glass of Champagne with my friends. It all seems rather silly to me. I am now hoping all the wonderfully creative people I work with will also be upgraded.

It's the last week before Christmas and it is now make or break time. We are hoping for the last minute rushes and we shall all be working right up until Christmas Eve. Even though we are exhausted we always manage to arrange to have a Christmas meal together, sometimes in an expensive restaurant, of which there are plenty to choose from, that is if it has been a really prosperous time. If it has been a lean year we still go out for dinner but try to find a more economical venue but interesting all the same. We celebrate together regardless of religious persuasion, after all we are just like a family.

When the time comes to actually pack up for the Christmas break you feel as though a great weight is beginning to be lifted from your shoulders and a light hearted sensation begins to creep over you. It's time to say goodbye to Karrie, Jane, Lorna, Tilly, Parish and indeed all my friends at the Market who have helped to make the year so eventful. The overwhelming feeling is to be at home with family and friends, then Christmas will really begin.

Another year has disappeared, the A, B and C's have been discontinued so we are hoping that next year will bring more security and happier times for everyone

P.S.. We have just discovered Tango lessons!

THE MARKET ADVENTURES OF DOROTHY PICTURES

Every day there is an amazing sight to see, they come to display their feathers like exotic birds and, of course, they have a captive audience – it is this atmosphere which I have tried to capture in the book.

Each year brings its joys and sorrows but the compassionate, funny, eccentric traders who are the heart and soul of the Market always try to find an answer one way or another.